Yours For Peaceful Comes
Mrs. L. D. Avery=Stuttle

Making Home Peaceful

SEQUEL TO
"MAKING HOME HAPPY"

BY

MRS. L. D. AVERY-STUTTLE
Author of "Making Home Happy," Etc.

PACIFIC PRESS PUBLISHING COMPANY
Mountain View, Cal.

Regina, Sask., Can.   Portland, Or.   Kansas City, Mo.

Republished by:
A. B. Publishing, Inc.
Ithaca, Mi 48847
Cover Art:
James Converse
copyright 1997
by A. B. Publishing

PREFACE

IN theory, home without happiness is as unthinkable as heaven without bliss. But earthly homes are often imperfect. That peace of mind, and heart, and life, which is essential to unalloyed enjoyment, is sometimes lacking. Such a lack is fatal if allowed to continue; but, fortunately, it is not irremediable.

In this book it has been the supreme purpose of the author to show the reader, by means of a happily conceived object-lesson, how the true spirit of the ever-blessed Christ-love can be given tangible expression in every-day home life, and how the incoming of that love will transform a joyless abode into a happy home. Too often this must be accomplished through the ministry of pain and sorrow. Far better to read and heed a lesson of love and peace, and of escape from unloveliness and strife, such as is so plainly and clearly set forth in these pages.

To be forewarned is to be thrice armed. For this

reason, such an object-lesson as the making of a home that is full of strife a blessed haven of peace and content is valuable to set before all members of every household. Both the homes that are and those that are to be, will profit thereby. Those that have happiness and peace will appreciate and prize this blessing the more, and those that have it not will desire it. The hearts of them that are apt to strive will be tempered, and softened, and beautified, and they who are already sweet and kind will be strengthened and perfected in every good and lovely trait.

PUBLISHERS.

CONTENTS.

CHAPTER IX

CHAPTER X

CHAPTER XI

CHAPTER XII

CHAPTER XIII

CHAPTER XIV

CHAPTER XV

CHAPTER XVI

CHAPTER XVII

CHAPTER XVIII

CHAPTER XIX

List of Illustrations.

CHAPTER I

WAITING FOR JIMMIE

"I DON'T see how in the world we can do it, Jimmie!" exclaimed young Mrs. Beardsley, peevishly. "I suppose I am willing to do as much for your father as daughters-in-law generally are expected to do; but there's a limit to everything."

"I know there is, Ellen; but it seems hard, now poor Jennie's gone, to leave him in the old house alone."

There was a suspicious huskiness in James Beardsley's voice and a look in his eyes that his wife knew very well meant an earnest determination to carry his point. Nevertheless, hers was a nature that could

11

not readily yield, even when her conscience told her she was in the wrong.

"Well, the fact is, James,"—Mrs. Beardsley always called her husband "James" when she wished to be impressive,—"the fact is, we have no place to put him. Mother has the west room, and I had intended to let Reginald have the front bedroom upstairs; but if Father Beardsley must come, why, there's an end of it."

"I am not willing to have father stay all alone, Ellen. I could not sleep at night and know that I had refused him a home in his old age. I know it's hard for you, but——"

"Yes, it *is* hard," whimpered Mrs. Beardsley, dashing away a tear; "but I can do it, of course; I always expect to give up for other people. Our son can sleep in the garret, I suppose,—poor boy! With Flossie and the baby, I have my hands full enough now, seems to me, without——" and Mrs. Beardsley finished her argument with a sob.

Jimmie Beardsley was in a quandary—some people called him "Jimmie" yet. He knew very well what his duty was; and, though his inclination and duty pointed in the same direction,—for he dearly loved his father,—he knew well that it would be like rowing against the tide to oppose his wife, whose will was usually law with him. But duty triumphed. He would not leave his old father alone. He would bring him to his own home without delay. How lonely he must be without Jennie!

Poor Jennie! she had faithfully stayed with her old father year after year, waiting upon him devotedly; nursing him when he was ill; and being eyes for him when the relentless hand of Time had thrown a mantle of blackness over him, and touched the gentle, kindly eyes with his cruel fingers, and with the breath of his thin lips had blown the light of the sun all but out of them. "My little Jennie," as the old deacon fondly called her, had stayed on after the others had gone,—stayed on, until the dark-eyed man who had in vain urged her to come and make his "home happy" had forsaken her,—stayed until the roses had faded from her cheek, and the light from her eyes; and now she was gone. The letter that the deacon had scrawled with trembling hand, and almost sightless eyes, had told them all about it, and it was this that had given rise to the conversation quoted above.

"It is strange the telegram informing us of Jennie's death could have been so delayed. Poor father!

I only hope he'll be contented here. O, if only I could have seen my sister once more!'' mused the sad-hearted man, to whom the news of his beloved sister's sudden death had come with crushing weight.

Mrs. Beardsley said no more. Argument, she knew, was of no avail. She must prepare for her added ''burden,'' as she looked upon it, and make the best of it.

That afternoon found James Beardsley on the way to Jonesville. On the train he had time for that quiet thought and reflection for which the hurried man of business and many cares seldom took a moment. But now he could think it all over—of his leaving the old farm so many years ago; of his subsequent marriage; of the steadfast faithfulness and devotion of his beloved Jennie; of his mother, so long since resting; of the death of their older sister under the sunny skies of India, her chosen field of labor for the Master; and of his brother Paul's unceasing service in the same far-off clime. Then he thought of his own unworthiness and unfaithfulness. He felt indeed like a prodigal son—a wanderer from his Father's house. The rush and worry of the years which had intervened between the present and the happy, careless days of his boyhood, had driven him farther and farther away from his Master.

James Beardsley closed his eyes, from which the tears trickled slowly, and was a boy again. He could hear once more his little sister's merry laugh as they romped together over the old haymow or chased the butterflies that flitted over the dewy fields of clover. He thought of his own sorrowful home-leaving; of his discontent and his longing for the great world; of his father's trembling farewell, and his ''God bless you, Jimmie;'' and of his rosy sister's silent tears as she said ''Goodby'' to her ''other self,'' as she called him. And, as he mused, his heart grew tender; and the first real prayer he had offered for many years rose to his lips. He had offered many formal prayers; but *this* was a prayer for mercy and forgiveness, and for strength to lead a more unselfish life.

It was sunset of the next day before the brakeman called the familiar ''Jonesville!'' How natural it sounded! O, if only Jennie were at the old station to meet him! How well he remembered her rosy cheeks and her brown eyes. How she used to like the pretty ''pep'mints'' that Jack Somerville gave them. O, those days! Was it possible that he was a bearded man, wise and hard-hearted from rough contact with the great world? an innocent boy yesterday—a man to-day!

James Beardsley walks along the familiar streets as if in a dream. How low and dumpy the stores and business offices look! The few people in the streets and sitting in the doors stare at him; they see that he is a stranger, and strangers are something out of the ordinary in Jonesville. Ah! there is the old house; how familiar the slim poplars look that stand before the gate! Jennie and he used to play they were giant sentinels. A strange dog hurries out, and growls ominously. Look! there is his father. He is sitting on the old veranda, with his head, snowy with age, bowed on his hand. The last rays of the autumn sun are shining upon him through the rent places in the tangle of vines at his back. The old man starts up at the sound of the dog, and an eager, questioning look comes into his dim eyes. He can just discern the form of a man, but he does not know him. It is a poor, broken-down old man that our traveler finds "waiting for Jimmie."

"Father!"

"Yes, Jimmie!" and the strong man throws him-

WAITING FOR JIMMIE

self on his knees at his father's feet; and, as the old deacon's fingers twine among the jetty locks caressingly and smooth the broad forehead tenderly, James Beardsley forgets but that he is a child again.

CHAPTER II

KNEW you'd come, Jimmie; Jennie said, just before she shut her pretty eyes, that Jimmie'd come. But O, the days have seemed so long since she left me! You're all I've got now, Jimmie; 'tisn't anywise likely I shall ever see Paul again, till I meet him and mother and Emma and little Jennie up yonder."

"Don't speak so, father! you'll live a long, long time yet. Let's see; you're only eighty-four! that's not old,—no, that's not old,—and I've come for you; we'll be ready in a day or two to go back to Harrisburg. I've a large house, you know,—built an addi-not since you were out there, that must be as much as twelve years ago."

"Yes, Jimmie, twelve years ago come Christmas. I remember your Regie was a little bit of a chap then. But I didn't stay long enough to get acquainted with Ellen."

20

"Well, Ellen's a good-hearted girl; I hope you'll like her. Reginald's a fine boy, fourteen years old and past—large for a boy of his age; and Flossie's four,—how you'll love that child! she reminds me of sister Emma, with her great blue eyes and sweet face. Then baby Bess is as cunning as can be. You'll not be lonesome—you can't be, as I see."

It must be confessed, however, that James Beardsley felt some misgivings, for he knew his wife's natural distaste for added burdens, and he remembered their conversation on the arrival of his father's letter. Then as he thought, in spite of himself, of Reginald's boisterous, ungracious manners, he experienced a certain sadness of heart. His father had grown so childlike, so trusting, so unsuspicious, so affectionate, that he felt sure the first unpleasant word would cause him great grief.

"But, Jimmie," replied the old deacon, "don't you think the housekeeper can manage me nicely? Eben—that's Jet's boy—does the chores; he's been staying here with his grandmother ever since Jennie was sick. I haven't long to stay, and seems as if I couldn't leave the old home. Why, when it's still in the evening, and the crickets chirp in the grass, and I catch the sweet scent of the hay in the east meadow, I declare, Jimmie, I can see you all—mother, and Paul, and Emma, and the twins. I suppose I'll have to go, though seems to me I could get along a while yet with Mrs. Burns and Eben.''

''But, of course, you can't stay here any longer, father; I couldn't leave you to the tender mercies of a housekeeper, though Mrs. Burns is probably well enough. I must step into the kitchen and see her, and ask about Tot and Jet and all the rest. I've been so driven with business, and so neglected Jennie's letters, that I suppose the poor girl grew discouraged for she didn't write me much about the old neighbors along at the last. I see my own neglect now and I'm *so* sorry I didn't answer her last, long, loving letter—poor Jennie!''

Reader, is this the experience of any of us? Did we ever neglect to answer the *last* letter till the hand that penned it was still and cold, and the clods of the valley fell with their mournful echo over the dear one whom we so loved and so neglected?

''Good evening, Mrs. Burns!'' exclaimed the visitor, stepping into the kitchen and extending his hand to the motherly-looking little woman who stood washing dishes at the table. We would have recog-

"WHAT! DON'T TELL ME THIS IS JIMMIE BEARDSLEY!"

nized Mrs. Burns at once. She was a trifle grayer, a little stouter—that was all. The good-natured, peaceful face seemed still young and fresh; for Mrs. Burns was not, and had never been, a woman who allowed the cares and burdens of this life to gall and worry her. A Christian she was and had been for many years; and this was the secret of the bright, cheery smile that always seemed at home on her face. Hearing the strange voice at her side, she turned suddenly.

"What! don't tell me this is Jimmie Beardsley!" she exclaimed, wiping her hands hastily and giving her visitor a cordial salutation. "Why I never thought of you as anything but a boy. It's been years and years since you left Jonesville, hasn't it? My! how Tot would like to see you."

"Where is Tot now, Mrs. Burns? I'd like to meet her, and talk over old times. Let's see—she was a little younger than Jennie and I were."

"She's living over in Edenville. Three children, now, Tot's got," chattered the motherly little woman. "She and her husband are the main pillars of the church over there. Thank the Lord, they're Christians. I hope, Jimmie, your feet are placed firm on the Rock of Ages, though I don't s'pose I need to ask, hardly—any one with such a father."

"I am quite free to confess, Mrs. Burns," interrupted Jimmie, for the conversation was growing a little too personal for an uneasy conscience, "that I have not at all lived up to my privileges; but I am sure the Lord has not forsaken me. Where is Jet, may I ask?"

"The dear boy died three years ago; but he died a Christian, and that means a good deal. I remember his last words—'Peace like a river.' O, I tell you, Jimmie,—I'll have to call you Jimmie yet, I guess,—nobody but a Christian can have real peace in life or satisfying peace in death."

"I remember now, Jennie wrote me about it. I suppose you have his boy with you?"

"Yes, he lives with me. Eben's a pretty good boy; looks a good deal as Tot used to. But you haven't told me anything about your family."

Mrs. Burns was not satisfied until she had received a minute description of each member of James Beardsley's family; and, finally, when he excused himself and returned to the sitting-room with his father, the motherly voice of Mrs. Burns rang after him: "I'm dreadful glad to hear about your folks, Jimmie. I hope they're all travelin' the way of peace."

That night James Beardsley slept in the little old room hallowed by many tender memories,—the room which was once his brother Paul's, and, which, later, came to be his own. As his weary head sought its pillow and memory became busy with scenes of the past, it was the strong, kindly voice of the old housekeeper, which was the last sound he heard save the monotonous chirping of the crickets and the loud ticking of the clock in the hall:

> "When peace like a river attendeth my way,
>   When sorrows, like sea-billows, roll;
>   Whatever my lot, Thou hast taught me to say,
>   'It is well, it is well with my soul.' "

CHAPTER III

____

A PEEP INTO THE BEARDSLEY HOME

LET us take a peep into the home of James Beardsley, in the little city of Harrisburg, after his departure for Jonesville, and listen for a few minutes to the conversation of its inmates. We will take a seat in the corner of the dining-room, for the family are at the breakfast-table. The dining-room is large and pleasant, and opens into the cozy sitting-room from one side and into the parlor and library from another. James Beardsley had been a merchant for a number of years, and his business was steadily growing; for he was strictly honest, temperate, and friendly with every one.

It is evident, this morning, that something of unusual interest is about to happen. Mrs. Beardsley sits at the head of the table, pouring the coffee. Upon either cheek there is a bright spot, which tells of unwonted excitement. Grandmother Sharpe, Mrs. Beardsley's mother, sits at her right; Reginald is at the foot of the table; while four-year-old Flossie, everybody's darling,—golden-haired Flossie, a cripple from her birth,—sits very near her mother at the left. Baby Bessie is asleep in her crib, much to Mrs. Beardsley's relief; for the little one has been restless and uneasy all night.

"Well, I suppose this day marks the end of my freedom," said Mrs. Beardsley, with a sigh that was intended to impress her hearers as very pathetic.

"Now, see here, Ellen; I hope you ain't goin' to be run right over the first thing!" exclaimed Grandmother Sharpe, with an ominous snapping of her black eyes. "But *I* needn't say nothin'; I expect *my* opinions won't amount to nothin', after this," she continued, in a grieved manner.

"Well, you know how it goes," complained Mrs. Beardsley; "I said all I dared against his bringing his father here, in the first place, but you know just how set Jimmie is. I wouldn't mind it so much, but the old man's nearly blind, and that means no end of bother."

"I say, mother," called Reginald, in a high voice, "have I got to give up my new room to Grandfather

Beardsley? I needn't, need I? won't the little room over the kitchen, where I used to sleep, be good enough for him? He can't see anything, anyway; and, if I've got to help father down at the store after school, I'm going to have a good room. I ought to have that much.''

"I said all I could, my dear, to your father," said Mrs. Beardsley, blandly (Reginald, her first-born, was clearly the idol of her heart), "but you know how it is. Never mind, dear; if pa's willing, we'll let you have our room, and we'll take the smaller bedroom in the wing."

"I don't want your room! I want the front one. I'm going to have a good room, and that settles it!" at which his mother said no more.

"Well, ma," continued Reginald, as he helped himself to another cake, "do you want me to help you fix the old man's room up? I can, if you say so, before I go down to the store," he continued in a condescending manner. Reginald was always more unruly and disagreeable when his father was away.

"Is papa coming home to-day, gran'ma?" queried little Flossie, who had been listening intently to the conversation, with a troubled look on her sweet, pale face.

"Yes, Flossie, to-day," answered Grandmother Sharpe, with an unconscious modulation of her shrill tones. Everybody spoke softly to little Flossie; even Reginald forgot his usual imperious style when he spoke to his crippled sister. Something was wrong with her spine, and Flossie had never walked.

It hardly seemed that these two could be brother and sister, so utterly unlike were they in both disposition and feature: Reginald, with his keen black eyes and raven hair; Flossie, with eyes as blue as the May skies and ringlets like spun gold: Reginald, proud, imperious, selfish, overbearing, impulsive; Flossie, gentle, loving, tender-hearted, patient: the latter, old and womanly beyond her years; the former, vain, reckless, and fond of putting on the airs of a young man.

When breakfast was over, Mrs. Beardsley and Reginald repaired to the chamber to make the final decision as to which room was to be "sacrificed" to Grandfather Beardsley.

"I tell you, mother," said Reginald, decidedly, "this little bedroom over the kitchen's just the thing. Of course, there's not much of a view from the window, but he's 'most blind,—he couldn't see it if the view was ever so grand."

"I know, Regie; but I'm awfully afraid your father will object to that. You see there's only one window, and that can't be raised easily."

"Yes, I know; but old folks are always cold, and he'll not want his window open. Besides, I'm bound to have that front room myself."

Reginald

"Well, if your pa objects too strongly, you can have our bedroom, and we'll take the one in the wing,—though I did want that for company."

"I told you once I didn't want your room!" snapped the selfish lad. "It's queer a fellow's got to fight for every privilege he has! I'm getting old enough to have my own way part of the time, and I hope people will begin to understand it pretty soon. I want the room I've got, and I'm going to keep it. Can I have that dresser for my room? this

Flossie

little place will be crowded with it—and that rug, too?''

Mrs. Beardsley did not even make an effort to reprove her son, or to correct his domineering and disrespectful conduct. She seemed entirely unmoved by these words, which, had they been spoken by another, would have exasperated her beyond control.

How the selfish boy could persuade his mother that the rug, because it happened to be bright and pretty, could possibly take up more room than a plainer one, I can not imagine; but certain it is that his arguments prevailed, and, as a result, it was a very plainly and poorly furnished little room that was at last pronounced ready to receive Grandfather Beardsley.

Perhaps you may be somewhat surprised to learn that our friend, James Beardsley, his wife Ellen, and her mother, Grandmother Sharpe, were all members of the church, and that they had been for many years. To join the church had seemed to them the correct thing to do, from more than one point of view. In the first place, all the better class of people in Harrisburg were church-members and church-goers; the Willoughby's and the Green's belonged to the church, and they were the wealthiest people in the city. To be sure, Mr. Green was not a strictly temperate man, but, then, he was considered eminently respectable. And, certainly, if the better class were church-members, it would hardly do to be outside the fold, they reasoned. They wanted to live good, moral lives, of course; they would like to attend church, and felt perfectly willing to throw a few coppers into the contribution-box every Sabbath, to help lift a little on the church debt. So there seemed to be but one thing to do—to join the church. But clearly James Beardsley and his wife were growing more and more worldly every year. Sometimes, it must be confessed, he would find himself comparing his own home life with that of his godly father's, in the years long gone by. He did not mean to be a hypocrite, but he was startled now and then when the blessed Spirit gave him a clearer view of his own heart. Sometimes, too, of late, he trembled for his son. He dimly remembered the time when his dear brother Paul had been led to the very brink of ruin by bad companions. Harrisburg was no exception to other places. Temptation lurked on every corner. Some of the very boys whom he had once thought fit playfellows for Reginald, he had himself seen smoking cigars, and he had heard his own boy occasionally use language which certainly could not be denominated as choice. All this had troubled him much.

CHAPTER IV

―――

GRANDPA'S NEW HOME

JAMES BEARDSLEY had spoken to his wife about this; but she had only remarked that, of course, "boys would be boys," and had objected decidedly to Reginald's being "preached at." So he had thought best to say no more about the matter, fondly hoping that time or age and experience would lead the lad to correct his bad habits. Vain hope! As the days flew by, he appeared to develop a growing taste for the society of the worst element in Harrisburg. Not only so, but complaints kept coming to his parents about his conduct in school. More than once of late they had received notes from his teachers to the effect that he was causing them much trouble. To these Mr. Beardsley had replied in person, asking that patience and forbearance be exercised with his son, for the sake of the mother. And so a kind of peace—though really more toleration than peace—was maintained. But Reginald could scarcely endure even his mother's occasional feeble remonstrance.

Yet James Beardsley and his wife, especially the latter, thought—as thousands of others who adopt the same policy in the management of their children think—that they were doing right, that their way was the best. O, had they only hidden themselves behind Christ, and let Him lead them! had they listened to His voice when He spoke to them! But they were too wise in their own eyes to be taught by the great Teacher, who never made a mistake, nor appointed one task that did not need to be done, nor assigned one lesson that did not need to be learned. O, had they hidden behind Christ, as the engineer hides behind his headlight,—himself in the shadow, —then would the great, strong light have shone upon the track ahead, revealing all the obstacles in the way, and beaming ever brighter as they approached them.

Like Mr. and Mrs. Beardsley, how often we place ourselves before the great Headlight; and then what follows?—Why, we are bodies of darkness; we throw our own shadows on the track, and it is so dark that we can not see to guide our train. Then, when we make terrible mistakes,—mistakes in the guidance of the precious souls given into our keeping,—we make such ado, and moan and cry out against Providence with so loud a voice that we fail to hear the still, sweet tones of our Pilot, who longs for us to listen to His teaching. And so, year after year, our train, with its precious freight, rushes on and on into the midnight blackness of our own shadows, until at last death comes and takes it into his charge, and our loved ones into his keeping, and we see them hurled over the precipice into eternal ruin. We know then that it is too late. We might have kept them back from destruction, but we saw not the danger. Our own baleful shadows eclipsed the brightness of the shining light, and we could not see the ruin ahead. We were like Eli, whose example stands like a lighthouse on the shores of time, warning us to shun the rocks upon which were stranded hopes as fair as ours.

We—there are two classes of us—have been taking two different paths. One is the path of cold, hard formalism, devoid of all appearance of affection —the path where bloom no sweet flowers; where the harsh word and the tones of unkindness are often heard, and the rod of correction is used without love. Such a path was that chosen by James Beardsley's father, Deacon Beardsley, in those early days before the voice of God spoke to him and softened and made tender his hard heart. The other path is gay with flowers, but they are poisonous; the songs of revelry and mirth sound loud; the tones of faithful reproof are never heard, and the voice of prayer is silent. Frightful chasms are on all sides; destruction is before, and desolation and lamentation are behind; but the hand that is upon the throttle of the engine is palsied; the ear is deaf, the eye blind, the Headlight obscured.

"Down brakes!" shouts the watchman. But the cry is all unheeded until it is too late,—the fatal leap is taken.

But there is another road. Mothers, shall I tell you about it? Fathers, will you invite the Holy Spirit to point it out to you? Teachers, do you want to take this better road, with your precious freight of human souls? It is a narrow path, but flowers of love and kindness grow along its track. Nothing but the voice of gentleness and the tones of kindness are heard; love reigns supreme. Dangers there are,—there is no path that is free from them,—but the hand that guides the engine is firm, the eye is open, the ears are not stopped, the mighty Headlight shines clear and bright, and we can hear the voice of the great Leader saying, "This is the way, walk ye in it."

At last, just as the clock was striking twelve, the rumble of wheels was heard on the gravel walk, and Grandmother Sharpe, glancing from the window, announced hastily:

"James is comin', Ellen; the old man's got his trunk. Dear me! he acts like he might be stone blind. Wall, I declare for't!"

"Well, Jimmie, you've come at last!" exclaimed Mrs. Beardsley, a look of relief coming into her face. "I've worried about you; we rather expected you yesterday. This is Father Beardsley, I suppose," she rattled on without waiting to hear the gentle-voiced old man's reply.

"Yes, Ellen, and he's very tired. You'd better give him a cup of something hot, and let him lie down till dinner's ready."

"There," thought Mrs. Beardsley, "I've got to begin waiting on him already;" and, as she handed the meek-faced old man a cup of hot drink, she ungraciously remarked that she was "tired enough to drop."

"Wall, James, I declare for't!" put in Grand-

"James Is Comin', Ellen!"

mother Sharpe; "Ellen ain't done a thing but worry ever since you went away."

"That's too bad, I'm sure, grandmother," said Mr. Beardsley, pleasantly.

"I told her you'd likely got delayed, and not to worry; but *my* words don't seem to amount to nothin', any more," continued the old woman.

Jealousy grew and thrived as naturally in the soil of Grandmother Sharpe's heart as weeds in the garden. Her one complaint was that no one cared for her opinions or heeded her advice. That gentle manner, that utter forgetfulness of self, which is the sweet product and growth of years of meekness and Christian unselfishness, was a stranger to her. And it needs the abiding grace of Christ in large measure patiently to endure the continual goading and pricking and rasping caused by contact with such natures as these. And of this—the sustaining grace of Christ—never was there a more needy household.

"Where's Reginald?" inquired Mr. Beardsley, "and Flossie, and the baby?"

"Regie's gone fishing with the boys; there wasn't any school this afternoon. I didn't want him to go, —I knew he was needed at the store,—but he *would*

go.   Baby's asleep, and I presume Flossie's dozing
in her wheel-chair.''

"Here's Flossie, mama; has my papa come?''
chirps a soft voice from the sitting-room,—sweet
music to the lonely old man, on whose sensitive heart
the sharp tones and ungracious words of his daughter-
in-law and her mother had fallen like lead.

"Come and get Flossie!'' and in a moment two
strong arms were around the tiny form, and Flossie
was clasped close to her father's loving heart, in
which his gentle, helpless little daughter occupied
a large place.

"This is Grandpa Beardsley, Flossie; kiss him,
dear,'' said her father, still holding her tenderly.

Deacon Beardsley reached out his arms, and took
the child upon his knee; and, while the golden curls
lay against his cheek, he whispered, in a husky voice:
"Grandpa can't see you very plain, my darling, but
he can hear your sweet voice, and feel your soft little
hands; and when he's not so tired, grandpa'll tell you
lots of nice stories.''

Now Flossie's one desire was to hear about angels.
It mattered little of what the story treated; if only
"angels'' bore a prominent part, she was altogether
satisfied.   So she at once put in her plea:

" 'Bout the angels? Will you tell Flossie 'bout the pretty angels?'' Then remembering that grandpa had said he couldn't see very plainly, she added, sympathetically:

"Can't you see, grandpa? you's got eyes!'' laying a tiny finger over the old man's eyelids. The child was perfectly at home on the deacon's knee. "Can't you see? Flossie's so sorry.''

"Not much, little one, not much; but I'll see sometime, and then Flossie can walk.''

"Dear me!'' fretted Mrs. Beardsley, appearing in the door to announce dinner; "that child is always dreaming, and now she'll be worse than ever. Here, James, do manage your father; I don't know how. Lead him over to this side of the table.''

"Where's Janet, Ellen?''

"O, she had a headache, and went home this morning, and left me with everything on my hands. I sent Reginald with the wash over to Mrs. Mallery's —I couldn't bear to have the muss in the house to-day. Baby kept me awake almost all night,—I'm worried about that child, Jimmie,—she doesn't seem at all well.''

"O, I guess she'll come out all right, Ellen; I wouldn't worry."

"No, you wouldn't worry; you never worry, especially when 'twould be a relief to me if you only would."

"I wanted her to give the baby some castor-oil and put a poultice on her stomach, but she wouldn't hear to me. If the baby's sick and dies, I can't be blamed. Nobody cares for my advice no more," remarked Grandmother Sharpe, watching grandpa, to see how he took that item of news. But Deacon Beardsley ate his dinner in silence, wondering if things had always been like this at Jimmie's.

"Come, Ellen," said Mr. Beardsley, after the deacon had retired to the sitting-room with Flossie; "I suppose father'd like to go to his room. Which one have you fixed up for him?"

"O, one up-stairs," answered Mrs. Beardsley, evasively, assuming a careless manner, though she had been inwardly dreading to hear her husband ask this question.

"Which room?"

"The one where Regie used to sleep."

"You don't mean that little den over the kitchen!" exclaimed Mr. Beardsley.

"CAN'T YOU SEE, GRANDPA? YOU'S GOT EYES!"

"Yes I do!" snapped his wife, defiantly; "it's good enough, too!" But she winced under the indignation of her husband's eyes.

"I supposed you were going to prepare the front chamber for him, Ellen," remonstrated Mr. Beardsley, making a perceptible effort to control his rising temper and keep back the hasty words which sprang to his lips. "I will see the room before he goes up, Ellen;" and he hastened from the dining-room, slowly followed by his wife.

"You don't mean to put my father into this room! it can't be possible! It's the closest, dingiest, stuffiest, unpleasantest room in the whole house. I didn't think it of you, Ellen," and James Beardsley's voice was full of reproach and scorn.

Mrs. Beardsley could better endure her husband's anger than his scorn, and she replied, hotly: "Well, I hope you have exhausted your list of adjectives. I'd like to know what better I can do! I ought to have the wing room for company,—you know that, —and Regie shall not give up his for anybody. Poor boy! he has few enough pleasures and comforts."

"Few enough that he doesn't have," thought Mr. Beardsley; but he only said, sternly, glancing out of the window: "I see it's half past two by the town

4

clock. By three o'clock I shall expect you to have made what changes are necessary in this front room. I'll send Mrs. Mallery over to help you. There goes Bill Wells,—I'll ask him to help me set father's trunk up here in his room.''

Mrs. Beardsley knew that further remonstrance was useless, so she took refuge in tears, and went slowly down-stairs. She knew this meant giving up their room to Reginald, and depriving her of the cherished ''spare room,'' which only increased her feeling of ill will toward the innocent old man who was the cause of all her trouble.

It was nearly three o'clock; Mrs. Beardsley and Mrs. Mallery were still busy preparing the front chamber, and making the changes that Mr. Beardsley had determined should be made. Mrs. Beardsley was doing the work most ungraciously, and under continual mental protest. She was just wondering what Reginald would say, when she heard his step in the front hall. The next moment his voice rang out sharp and clear: ''Mother! hurry up and get me some dinner; I want one of these fish cooked— I've got some beauties! Come; I'm 'most starved. Has father come?'' Then she heard him ascending the stairs, two steps at a time. "Hello! what's this? I thought I was to have this room."

"Well, dear, your father didn't like it, so I had to make the change. You can't feel worse about it than I do. But you shall have our room. I'll fix it up nice for you, and we'll take the smaller one."

"A fellow'll have to stand it, I s'pose, though I don't like to give up for other folks," he scowled, as he came bounding down the stairs, entirely unmindful of the sacrifice his parents were making for him.

Flossie sat curled up in grandpa's arms; and the deacon was in the middle of a story that used always to awaken the admiration of the "twins," years and years ago.

"Why, little Flossie," he was saying, while the tiny form cuddled up to him closer still, "it doesn't seem a bit more than last week since I used to tell your own papa and Aunt Jennie that story;" and the dim old eyes grew dimmer still, as he brushed a tear away. "I didn't always do right by the little ones; but that's all past now, and whereas I was blind, now I see," said the old man, thoughtfully. He never ceased to find places where his favorite text would fit in appropriately.

"Was Aunt Jennie your little girl? Tell me about her, grandpa, please. Why, here's Regie!"

"Hello, Floss; hello, grand'ther! I suppose you've come to stay at our house, have you? I hope you aren't deaf,"—raising his voice to a higher pitch,— "I hope you aren't deaf as well as blind. I hate to talk to deaf people,—strains my throat."

The poor old man, thus rudely awakened from his sweet dream of the past, made some answer, as best he might, to the thoughtless boy, while Flossie slid down from his knee, and crept painfully into her wheel-chair; for grandpa looked so white and pale she thought he must be tired.

And so this was life at Jimmie's. O, how he longed for a quiet corner in his old home again!

"Poor grandpa!" she said, softly; "do your eyes ache, grandpa?"

"No, no, little girl, not my *eyes*. Why do you ask, Flossie?"

" 'Cause you can't see,—poor grandpa!"

Everybody said that little Flossie Beardsley was a strange child. Perhaps it was on account of her deformity, which, of course, made it out of the question for her to play the ordinary games of childhood with the children of the neighborhood; or perhaps it was because of the ministry of pain, with its purifying, softening influence, which had the effect of developing and ripening the spirit of the child, until she seemed almost a woman in her gentle thoughtfulness for the needs of others.

Born to a life of sorrow and suffering, to days of weakness and nights of weariness, the frail flower seemed only to give out the more perfume. Patiently enduring the pain incident to her helpless condition, —or, where it was too much for the brave little spirit, weeping silently,—the child was an example indeed. Grandfather Beardsley at once became a new object around which her heart-strings readily entwined. She thought it so dreadful because it was always dark to poor grandpa; and on account of her sympathy for him, she soon formed the habit of closing her eyes,—"playing blind," as she called it,—so she could understand how it seemed to grandpa.

The child had a great notion of playing by herself. She had large boxes filled to the brim with bright-colored pieces that had been given her; and she would sit in her chair hour after hour, and handle them all over, lovingly patting, with the frail, white little fingers, each particular piece, and pinning the choicest of them in turn on her dolls, where, in her imagination, they immediately underwent a miraculous change, and became at once transformed into fine new suits.

But of all things in the world, the sight of a beautiful sunset, gorgeous with its tints of purple and gold and scarlet, was most enjoyed by the crippled child. One evening when nature seemed trying to outvie itself in producing a magnificent panorama in the heavens, she sat in her little chair, regarding the scene with childish delight. Clasping her tiny hands in ecstasy, she exclaimed: "Do see, grandpa! I can look away over into God's country. We'll not be sick any more in God's country; we'll not feel bad any more there, and we can see the angels every day!"

Though Flossie was kind and loving toward all the children of the neighborhood, who sometimes came to the house to play with her, still, because they were rather boisterous and rough in their games, the frail, sensitive child generally preferred playing quite alone, or with her baby sister, Bessie; though Bessie could hardly be expected to enter very heartily into her quaint plays. However, there was one playfellow whom Flossie always welcomed. Even when she was in real pain, the gentle presence of little

Tim Mallery seemed to have a quieting, soothing effect upon her. Tim was the eight-year-old son of Mrs. Beardsley's washerwoman. He was a quaint little fellow, whose freckled face, clean and shining as soap and water could make it, was always beaming with a good-natured smile. His clothes were patched

Little Tim

until it was difficult to tell the original color, but they were scrupulously clean.

It never occurred to Mrs. Beardsley that it was her duty to make any effort whatever to better little Tim's condition, or in any way to help her poor neighbor out of the rut into which years of toil and grinding poverty had thrown her. Indeed, Ellen

Beardsley was only annoyed at the growing friendship between the children.

Kind and overindulgent to her own children, her
kindness did not extend over her own threshold.   For
the children of her neighbors she had neither gentleness
nor charity—especially for those of her poorer neighbors.   A professed Christian, indeed; but she had no
time for the exercises of those Christian graces, the
sweet fruits of the Spirit, without which the soul
grows colder and the heart harder day by day.

But, because Tim had nothing to do at home, nor
any toys to amuse himself with there, he often braved
Mrs. Beardsley's frowns and sharp words for the
pleasure of playing for half an hour with his little
favorite.

One morning after an unusually unkind greeting
from Mrs. Beardsley, who had told him that she did
not "want to be bothered" with him, and that it
was "time Flossie had her nap," she overheard a
snatch of conversation between the little daughter and
her early visitor, which should have been a lesson to
her, but which only served to irritate her the more.

"Say, Floss," began Tim, in the singularly soft
voice with which he always spoke to his gentle playmate, "your ma's just like our Spotty."

"Who *is* Spotty?" questioned Flossie.

"Why, she's the ma of them cunnin' little chickens I brought over here to show you a few weeks ago; 'cause you see, if there's any other chickens comes 'round, Spotty just pecks 'em."

"She doesn't hurt 'em, does she?" protested Flossie.

"I s'pose she does; anyway, it hurts me, awful, when she's cross to me, an' looks at me so with them black eyes—your ma, I mean. I wouldn't das't come over here at all, Flossie, only I like to play with you so!"

"Never mind, Timmie," exclaimed Flossie, alarmed at the thought of such a possible calamity; mama didn't mean to hurt you. Come, let's play school."

If you were to ask Mrs. Beardsley whom she loved —absolutely and entirely loved—and for whom alone she would uncomplainingly sacrifice her own comfort, who and who only occupied her thoughts by day and her dreams by night, she would answer, if she told you what she believed to be the exact truth, "My children—Reginald first, then Flossie and little Bessie." And she made every other love, every other condition of her life and the lives of the other members of her household, secondary to this. She loved

her husband, or at least it is to be so supposed, though
she rarely manifested any tenderness toward him;
and if his interests and Reginald's ever conflicted, it
was the self-willed lad who always received the favors
and concessions.

These little differences between Mr. and Mrs.
Beardsley became more and more frequent after the
arrival of the deacon, who was from the first a continual bone of contention between them. Reginald
shared his mother's spirit of rebellion at the coming
of the old deacon into their home, and James Beardsley began to feel more keenly than ever in his life
his own sad lack of the wisdom that comes from above.
He soon ceased to offer anything but the feeblest remonstrance to Reginald's disrespectful and unmanly
treatment of his grandfather and to his growing dislike of restraint. The lad knew that he had a never-
failing friend and ally in his mother; it mattered not
how much he needed the firm hand of restraint and
the earnest voice of remonstrance, Ellen Beardsley
never failed to enter a prompt protest, without waiting to be alone with her husband, if the remonstrance
was forthcoming. Yet, strange as it might appear,
the lad whom she so favored did not regard her

TROT, TROT, TROT, BACK AND FORTH, FLY THE LITTLE FEET
(See page 105)

wishes any more than those of any one else, if they conflicted in the least with his own.

And the misguided woman called this feeling for her children,—this feeling of resentment at any protest uttered on account of there waywardness,— "love." But did she love them wisely? Was she not yielding up to her children that place which belongs only to God? Was she not placing in the sanctuary of her heart an earthly idol, where Christ alone should bear rightful sway? It is always so whenever we attempt to substitute the false for the true,—whenever we concede to "the gift" that love which alone belongs to the Giver, whenever we place a poor, weak, erring mortal upon the highest throne of our affections, and give to him the first place, which belongs only to the Creator. Even baby Bessie was learning to manifest a distressing degree of temper if her wishes were not at once granted. But Mrs. Beardsley was blind and deaf to all these things.

"Isn't baby cunning!" she exclaimed one day at the dinner-table, when the tiny queen asserted her "rights" in louder tones than usual—she was crying for a pretty glass mug in this particular instance. "Isn't she cunning, James? Do see her little eyes flash! Never mind, James, *I'll* hand it to her; don't

you know she' won't let any one hand her a drink
but me? I believe that child's growing to look more
like me every day she lives. *She* doesn't intend to
be stepped on, *do* you darling?'' and the indulgent
mother quickly handed the child the desired object. Instantly the cries ceased; but the mug had
been too long delayed. The child was angry, and
would not easily be pacified. There was a quick
movement of the little arm, a crash, and Flossie's
mug, a cherished gift from grandpa, lay in fragments
on the smooth, hard floor of the dining-room. Deacon
Beardsley quietly repeated a verse of Scripture, as
it was his habit to do: " 'Even a child is known by
his doings, whether his work be pure, and whether
it be right.' ''

CHAPTER V

OF course, Flossie began to cry quietly. It was not her nature ever to make a noisy demonstration; but the hot tears rained down upon the white cheeks, and the pale lips quivered pitifully.

"Why Bessie!" exclaimed Mr. Beardsley.

"Now don't scold the child, James. She's not old enough to reason with, much less to punish, and I hope you'll remember it. Don't look at her so; there! I knew you'd have her crying. Come here, darling," reaching her arms for the angry infant, "papa sha'n't scold mama's baby! naughty papa!"

"I told you the child would break the dish, Ellen, if you gave it to her," said Mr. Beardsley, reproachfully.

"Yes, of course you told me!" snapped Mrs. Beardsley. "You are all the time croaking. You always refuse the children everything. Come quickly,

and gather up the pieces, Janet. Don't cry, Flossie;
mother'll get you another mug, prettier than this one.''

"Yes, but grandpa got me this, poor, blind
grandpa, and he can't see to get me another," moaned
Flossie.

"O, yes, I can, dear," said the deacon, consolingly,
glad of an opportunity to pour oil upon the troubled
waters. "Yes, I can, dear. 'Whereas I was blind,
now I see.' "

Grandmother Sharpe had been listening jealously
to the last part of this conversation. Deacon Beardsley had been a member of his son's household only
a few hours before she decided that he would be a
dangerous rival in Flossie's affections; and as the
months rolled by, she never lost an opportunity of
letting every one know that she considered him as such.

"It's dretful quare," she exclaimed pettishly, "the
children never seem to think anything of what *I* give
'em. My presents ain't sot no store by; nobody
cares for *me* no more in this house!"

"Now you've begun your usual tune!" exclaimed
Reginald, turning with a sneer toward his grandmother. "But I don't see what grand'ther means by
saying that whereas he was blind, now he sees, when
he's blind as a bat, and growing blinder every day,

—Scripture, I wouldn't wonder,—not much use playing the pious dodge here,'' and the heartless boy, unrebuked except by a stern glance from his father, left the room, while Deacon Beardsley thought: ''O what a change might be wrought in my poor son's unhappy household if cold formality might only give place to the blessed religion of Jesus Christ; and if the sweet charity that thinketh no evil, that suffereth long, and is kind, that vaunteth not itself, would but take the place of the love of self. Would to God that whereas they are blind, they might be able to see.''

''It does not seem possible that you have been giving us a picture of a *Christian* family—a fair picture!'' I hear somebody exclaim. No, not a picture of a *real,* but of a *professed,* Christian household. Real Christianity is as far removed from the false as the east is from the west. If there is a genuine —and let us thank God that there is—just so surely there is a counterfeit. The one is only a sham, a deception, a miserable make-believe. The light which it sheds is a fatal *ignis fatuus;* it allures and turns from the right path the poor travelers on the highway of life, only to lead them on to destruction and certain death. The other forms the foundation of every well-regulated household. It shines with a steady ray;

5

for the oil of love and kindness supplies the flame. The father of such a household is filled with the love of Christ, which continually seeks expression in kindly acts of love and tenderness toward the dear ones entrusted to his keeping by his loving heavenly Father.

But while he is kind and tender, he does not forget that he is filling the position of priest in his household. He is captain of the little barge for whose safe landing he is in a great measure responsible; and so, while the voice which commands the ship is gentle, it is steady and firm as a rock; and while the eye may be often wet with the tears of sorrow at the wayward course of some son or daughter, he does not allow it to become so dim that he can not see his chart and compass, or so dull that he can not follow the directions of his Guide-Book.

The mother of such a household is gentle and loving and true. Her children rise up and call her blessed. To them she is a counselor, a refuge, a ministering angel, a tender companion. But while she studies to minister to their comfort in every way that love can devise or true affection suggest, she withholds from them those hurtful pleasures that she knows will only bring days and nights of regret and sorrow, and years of remorse and shame. In every way will the Christian mother aid her husband in his duties, and seek to cheer and encourage him with sympathy and words of counsel. If he is the priest, she is the priestess; if he is the captain, she is the pilot.

And what shall I say of the children of an ideal Christian home? Surrounded from their babyhood with an atmosphere of love and peace, accustomed to look to father and mother for guidance and counsel, and never refused that love and tenderness which are the natural inheritance of every child born into the world, they come, in time, to take right views of life, and to choose—perhaps from force of circumstances and environment at first, but from intelligent and deliberate choice at last—that path of wisdom into which their feet were early placed by their godly parents.

"There are exceptions to this rule," you assert. Are there?—Well, perhaps; but Solomon made no mention of them. "Train up a child in the way he *should* go;"—that is, make *no* mistake in the training of your child,—"and when he is old, he *will not* depart from it." There you have the promise. You do *your* part, and God has pledged His eternal word as to the results.

"O, yes; but every one makes mistakes!" Ah,

there is the trouble. It is *our own* mistakes that cause the mischief; and then we blame the Lord for the results. If with reproof comes love; if with refusal to grant some cherished wish of the little one there is granted something else which is better; if with the rod of correction comes the tear of sympathy,— then, and then only, can we expect to bind our dear ones to our hearts with a threefold cord of love which can not be broken. That is the way the Lord deals with us, His erring children. He never refuses us anything without giving us something much better than what we ask for. He never chastens us but in love and pity, nor rebukes us but in mercy.

But this is an ideal Christian household; and James Beardsley's was not such. That deference which is the rightful heritage of gray hairs was not taught by precept nor by example.

The course that had always been taken by Grand-mother Sharpe was not one which would naturally inspire the respect and love of the children, nor the forbearance and filial cordiality of her daughter and her son-in-law. In fact, she had developed just that kind of disposition which, to James Beardsley, was particularly harassing. If any one mentioned a good deed done by some one else, Grandmother Sharpe was

ever ready with a querulous complaint that she was
not appreciated, and that what she had done was of
no account in the eyes of the family, for whom, as
she represented it, she constantly labored for naught.
The remotest word of affection or appreciation expressed toward the deacon was the signal for a torrent
of reproach and jealousy from the misguided woman.

If there is any place in life where the abiding
grace and wisdom of God are needed, it is in dealing
with such natures as these. You may be able to reason
with a *child;* but it is often impossible either to reason
with or to restrain these children with gray hairs
and wrinkled brows. Nothing but the transforming
grace of Christ can so remold and remake these unlovely characters as to form them into vessels of honor.
He can do the work that it is impossible for us to
do. With Him it matters little whether the vessel
be old or new, or whether the heart-temple be shattered
and in ruins, or corrupt and polluted. His grace
is sufficient; all He asks is an entrance; and He has
promised to make the hoary head a crown of glory.

CHAPTER VI

TOM AND REGINALD

AMES BEARDSLEY was becoming more and more alarmed every day over the waywardness of his son.

"It seems to me, Ellen, that something ought to be done with Reginald," he said one night to his wife. "Really, the boy is getting entirely out from under my control; and when I think that he has only just passed his fifteenth year, I am greatly distressed."

"Why, what has he been doing so terrible, Jimmie?" responded Mrs. Beardsley, fretfully; "seems to me he's just as likely a boy as any around here."

"Well, Ellen, I'll tell you; I guess I might as well. I thought I would keep it from you, but I think you ought to know."

"Dear me, Jimmie! come, out with it! don't keep me waiting any longer. Seems as if you delight in torturing me sometimes. I'm sure I wish *I* could bear the blame of everything Regie does that's wrong. I guess you forget the time when *you* were a boy."

"Wait, wait, Ellen! hear me!" exclaimed her husband, impatiently; "I ought to have told you before. You know last Tuesday night you and I supposed Reginald was at the store. I was called away early in the evening, and left him to help Tom Willis and Riggs behind the counter an hour or two, as I have often done, supposing he would be home at nine. You remember he did not come home till nearly eleven o'clock, and gave as an excuse that the customers kept coming in so he couldn't be spared. I thought it was strange at the time. Well, Tom told me the next day that Reginald left the store early in the evening, after making his boast that he wasn't going to be held in by the 'old man,' as he was pleased to call me, much longer. Tom said he imagined something was wrong from what the boy had hinted about a certain appointment; so he looked in at the window as he passed Reddy's Hotel on his way home. It's not a regular saloon, of course, but they sell liquor there, and, sure enough, there was *our boy*,—think of it, Ellen!" and her husband's voice quavered with emotion—"*our boy!* I tremble to think of him there at such an hour, and in such company! and he didn't

get home for nearly two hours afterward. Of course,
I don't suppose he visits such places very often yet,
but he was certainly there then, for Tom saw him.
Then there was the miserable lie he told us about it.
I repeat it, Ellen, *what* are we going to do?''

The face of Mrs. Beardsley was a study when her
husband stopped speaking. It grew white and scarlet in turn.

''And so you intend to criminate your own son,
do you, on the word of that worthless fellow!'' she
exclaimed, her thin lips white and bloodless, and
twitching with excitement. ''If I can have *my* way,
he'll be discharged to-morrow for concocting such lies
about his employer's son. He's just envious, I know
he is, because Regie took the prize in that spelling
contest last winter; he worked hard to get it himself;
and now he's trying to turn the poor boy's own father
against him. It's just out of pure spite—I know
it, James. If my boy is going to be persecuted so
at home, I guess he'll have to go to brother Earl's
to school, as he wants to. I think his uncle will at
least see that he is well-treated; and though it seems
as if the thought of having him away from home
would break my heart, I can not have him persecuted
so. Why, James,'' she continued, ''Reginald told us

why he was home late; he said he was busy at the store; and I, for one, prefer to take his word in preference to a stranger's. I *insist*, James, that you discharge that fellow!'' and Mrs. Beardsley began to sob convulsively.

''Why, Ellen! I can not think of such a thing. It would be most unjust. Besides he's not a stranger. Tom Willis is one of my most trusty clerks. He has served me faithfully for over five years; I can not discharge him. Would God my own son were as trustworthy as Tom Willis!''

''Call him trustworthy, if you want to,'' sobbed Mrs. Beardsley; ''you'll find him out after a while! I tell you plainly, if you do not discharge him at once, you will regret it;'' and in her heart the indignant and misguided woman determined that not a stone should be left unturned in the way of accomplishing her object; and from that time she began a series of petty persecutions against Tom Willis.

''I thought it my duty to tell you this,'' continued Mr. Beardsley; ''but I'm sorry now that I did so. I hoped that we might be able, together, to devise some way to save our poor boy from the snares of the devil; but you can't see it as I do,—you can't see his danger,—so I'm sorry I told you.''

"*I'm* not sorry you told me," echoed his wife, "I shall be on the outlook after this, and I shall see that Reginald is on his guard against this 'honorable' clerk of yours. I dare say he has spread his nice little story all over town. But as long as my dear boy has a mother, she will protect him."

James Beardsley's only reply was a deep sigh. He had hoped to have a sort of conference with his wife in regard to many matters. For a long time he had not felt satisfied with the careless way they were living. His godly father's careful walk and conversation had been a continual reproof ever since he had lived with them. He saw that the old deacon sadly missed the morning and evening worship to which he had been accustomed.

Sometimes as the shades of twilight gathered, and the stars—God's lamps—came out in the sky, the busy man had noticed a peculiarly sad expression come into the old man's calm, white face, and the lines on the noble forehead seemed to grow a little deeper, as he would call Flossie, and, holding the tiny form close to his heart, would sing, in a trembling voice, those blessed songs of Zion that James Beardsley so well remembered. They were the same that used to ring out from the old homestead among the hills at

Jonesville in years long past. Then to the man of many cares would rise a picture. It was of a quiet family group: father, mother, each with a little brown-eyed child—Jennie and Jimmie of the long ago—seated on the arm of the spacious rockers, while in imagination he could hear the manly tones of his brother Paul, and see the dewy tear spring to the eyes of his beloved elder sister, as they all joined in singing—

"Rock of Ages, cleft for me;
Let me hide myself in Thee."

At such times as these the Holy Spirit strove mightily with him. The time had been, years before, when he and his wife had first joined the church, that the family altar had been raised; but as he had always realized that there was more formality than heart religion about its services, he had yielded to her suggestions that family prayers be discontinued.

CHAPTER VII

ND so this wonderful means of grace, provided and ordained of God, had been neglected; and Mrs. Beardsley's children were growing up in a prayerless atmosphere. Sometimes, since his father had come to live with them, James Beardsley had suggested to his wife a return to the old customs; for the Spirit of God was touching his heart and making it tender. But whenever he attempted, in the remotest manner, to draw comparison between his present home and that of his childhood, he was always met with reproaches from his wife.

"Of course *your* father never made any mistakes, nor your mother, either, likely enough," she would say. "I don't see but I'm about as good as the ones who profess to be so perfect, and my family's just as good as my neighbor's."

Reader, are you forming an unfavorable opinion of this woman, a little of whose daily home life has been presented before you? Are you already judging her as a hot-tempered, hasty woman of the world, misguided and selfish in the extreme? Are you comparing her in your heart to some of your own acquaintances? Ah, let us be careful lest, in our search for some one to fit this unhappy character, we forget to look in the very place where possibly her face is reflected and her character duplicated—in *our own* selfish hearts.

I am not a pessimist, and I hope I shall not be called pessimistic when I say that there are many and many Ellen Beardsleys in the church of Christ to-day. With this, the great Founder of the Christian religion is not pleased. What *does* He want? O, He would purify and cleanse them, if they would only let Him! He wants them to open wide the doors, and let Him come in, with all His heavenly messengers—a glorious train. He invites you, me, every one, to exchange our selfishness for His charity, our impurity for His purity, our garments of filthy rags for His robe of righteousness. Many of us have learned that love and tenderness should rule every action in the home government; and so we immediately go to the other extreme, and blindly close our eyes to the foibles, and even to the grosser evils, of our children. Thus the tender twig grows almost hopelessly crooked; and the little branches, which might once have been trained to grow in beauty and symmetry by our side, become so deformed and twisted that nothing but a miracle of grace can ever make them anything but unsightly trees in the Master's vineyard.

Perhaps it would be well now to speak of the past life and character of Tom Willis, the young clerk who had been so unfortunate as to gain the hot displeasure of his employer's wife.

First, let me say that Mrs. Beardsley had no intention of being unjust to the young man. She really believed that he was maliciously telling falsehoods about her beloved son. She had so long refused to see any of his misdeeds that she could not persuade herself that her boy—her Regie, whom she looked upon with such pride, and in whom centered so many fond hopes—could be a common liar, and voluntarily associate with low fellows at the beer-table, she could not make herself believe this, even when she had the best of evidence—so effectual an anesthetic is selfishness.

Perhaps it was the fact that Tom's father had died a wretched, bloated drunkard, when Tom was only a small boy, that caused him to have an unspeakable horror of strong drink, and of everything connected with it. Perhaps it was the dying words of his mother, which with each succeeding year of his life seemed to ring louder and louder in his ears, that led him to watch with almost a brother's care the young son of his employer. Ah, how well he remembered that lonely night in dreary November, when his mother, his best earthly friend, had called him to her bedside, thrown her wasted arms about him, and pressed her white lips to his cheek, as she whispered with her last breath her dying request: "Promise me, Tom, my boy, promise me in God's name, you will not walk in the steps of your father. Promise me that by word and example you will lead every poor boy over whom you have any influence away from the accursed cup." That promise was made; and with a smile of peace, and a prayer that God would bless her boy, she had passed away.

Then there was ever before him that other night, black and horrible, which had been burned into his memory as with a hot iron, when his father lay upon his bed of straw, mad with the horrible delirium which rum had caused,—that broad forehead, once noble and lofty, marred as with the brand of Cain; those piercing eyes, which had once beamed with intelligence, now bleared and expressionless, or filled with an unspeakable horror; and that noble frame, once strong and active as a giant's, prostrate and writhing as if in the embrace of a serpent. With a shriek of agony, the tortured victim of the cup of demons had closed his eyes to earth forever.

Is it any wonder that Tom had a peculiar horror of the saloon and its accursed traffic? He had noticed the growing tendency of young Reginald to see evil associates; and, after pleading with him, and giving him as good advice as he knew how,—but all to no purpose,—he had determined, when he saw the young man at "Reddy's," to talk frankly with his employer, and tell him all about it. Little did he know the storm of wrath that he was calling down upon his head.

It was Monday morning—wash-day at James Beardsley's. Breakfast was just over, and Mrs. Sharpe was concluding her old-time remarks on the strangeness of the fact that nobody seemed to care anything for her, when Mrs. Mallery knocked hastily at the side door, and without waiting to be admitted, thrust her head, carefully wrapped in many folds of red woolen cloth, into the dining-room, and in her rich Irish brogue, announced: "It's mesilf that's laid up entoirely wid me neuralgy since this last cold snap, Mrs. Beardsley; and me bye, Tim, that's sick wid a high faver——''

"O, I know what you are going to say, of course; you can't do my washing to-day! I just felt sure something would happen, because I'm in an awful hurry!" exclaimed Mrs. Beardsley, fretfully. "It's always just so," she added. "I shall send Janet at once for Mrs. Poole. Really, Mrs. Mallery, I can not have such irregularity about my washings." At the mention of Mrs. Poole, the poor woman broke down entirely; she could barely live anyway, and felt that she could not afford to lose even the paltry earnings of one washing. So it was arranged that she take it home with her. Finally, as she started off with her heavy load, she paused long enough to explain that "rint was that high," and that with her own and Tim's doctor bill, she could barely live. "Me Timmy's a mighty slinder choild, an' I ofttimes faier I'll not kape him long," she concluded.

"The very idea!" exclaimed Mrs. Beardsley, with a sneer, as soon as her caller had departed; "the child's as tough as a bear! I'll risk him! It beats all and all how the silly woman humors that great freckle-faced, awkward child."

"Why, you know, Ellen, the boy is all she has

6

left since her 'poor mon,' as she calls him, died. I can't blame her," said Mr. Beardsley; "you know how you feel toward our children."

"As if, James,—as if *my* children could be compared to that horrid little Irish boy!"

"O mama, don't, please don't!" pleaded Flossie, whose tender heart was at once touched when she heard of her little favorite's illness. "Flossie does like Tim, 'cause——"

"You are spoiling that child, James, by encouraging her in choosing such low-bred associates," interrupted Mrs. Beardsley, haughtily. Mr. Beardsley's only reply was a quiet smile, while Grandmother Sharpe hastened to remark, in an injured manner, that she had her opinion, but of course nobody cared to hear what *she* thought.

Mrs. Beardsley had never liked Tim,—she did not like any children but her own,—and this occurrence and conversation only deepened her dislike for him. Consequently, a few days afterward, when the poor, pinched little face, whereon the much-ridiculed freckles stood out plainer than ever, appeared at the door, Mrs. Beardsley was decidedly irritated; but Flossie begged so hard for a half-hour's play with him that her mother gave a reluctant consent.

It was only a little while after the child had left that Mrs. Beardsley had occasion to pass a dresser where she was sure she had that morning left a five-dollar gold piece. The money belonged to Janet, the hired girl. A friend had called that morning and had left the money, which she had owed Janet for some time; and as Janet was gone that day, her friend had asked Mrs. Beardsley to hand it to her. Now it was gone. She called to mind at once that she had seen Tim in that room, near the dresser; for she had noticed the reflection of his pale, pinched face, with its big eyes, and the shock of yellow hair, in the mirror. Yes, she knew he had been in the room; and now the money was gone.

CHAPTER VIII

WHO IS THE THIEF?

THERE was but one conclusion to arrive at, in the mind of Ellen Beardsley—Tim Mallery had stolen the money, there was no mistake about it. Well, there was at least some satisfaction in the thought that she could now prove to her husband that her estimate of the child had been correct. However, she reasoned that there was a possibility that James might have picked it up at dinner time. Regie certainly had not touched it; he never did such things. She was careful to see that he had a liberal allowance of pocket-money; for she did not believe in boys of his age being cramped and hampered, and obliged to beg every cent of money they needed,—a policy she lived to regret with many a bitter tear. She finally decided she would say nothing about the matter until James and Regie came to supper. By this time she was more certain than ever that little Tim was the culprit, and had worked herself into quite a furor of "righteous indignation," as she termed it.

"James," she called, as soon as she heard her husband's step at the door, "did you see anything of that five-dollar gold piece I left on the dresser this morning? It was Janet's. I spoke about it at breakfast."

"Why, no, Ellen; why? Have you lost it?"

"Lost it!" exclaimed his wife, in a tragic manner; "of course I've lost it! And that isn't all,— that little Irish paragon of yours, Tim Mallery, has stolen it! I know it as well as if I had seen him take it."

"Why, you haven't asked Reginald yet; it may be possible he has it," suggested Mr. Beardsley.

"I know he hasn't it. He never does such things; he is not a common sneak-thief. O, I know who has it!"

If Mrs. Beardsley had noticed the peculiar expression that flitted over Reginald's face at that moment, as he exclaimed, doggedly, "I haven't got yer money!" she might not have been so sure of little Tim's guilt.

Mr. Beardsley noticed it; but warned by past experiences, he did not press his investigations further. By this time it began to dawn in Flossie's mind that her little playmate was being accused of something dreadful, of which the sensitive child knew instinctively that he was not guilty.

"O mama!" she pleaded, while the large tears ran down her cheeks; "Timmie didn't take the money. I *know* Timmie didn't take the money,—poor Timmie!"

"*Hush,* you naughty child!" commanded Mrs. Beardsley, impatiently, "he shall not play with you any more. There is no accounting for that child's queer taste," she added; and at these harsh words from her usually indulgent mother, little Flossie sobbed the harder, and refused to be comforted.

Even Reginald felt somewhat ill at ease, and went so far as to offer to show her his latest book, —a natural history with pictures of lions and tigers in it. This was an unusual proceeding on his part; but poor Flossie was so heart-broken at the direful prospect of never playing with little Tim again, that she only sobbed the more, refused to eat her supper, and, much to Mrs. Beardsley's annoyance, begged grandpa to rock her and tell her a story. Deacon Beardsley had learned to preserve a discreet silence at such times as this; and there was a look of patient

forbearance on the calm face, when Grandmother
Sharpe declared that it was "quare Flossie would
never let *her* rock her, or listen to any of *her* stories."
However, before leaving the table to minister to
Flossie, he remarked that as far as Timmie was con-
cerned, *he* thought the child entirely innocent; and
that it would be best to exercise a little of that blessed
charity which "thinketh no evil."

Mrs. Beardsley only bit her lip, and was silent;
but she determined, more from a desire to have her
own way and to prove that she was right, than from
any ill will, to see the child, and accuse him of the
theft, when, she had no doubt, he would immediately
acknowledge his guilt and return the money. More
than that, being so sure he had taken it, she decided to be very lenient,—she could afford to be,
when she had proved her point,—and refuse to take
the money when it was returned by the little culprit,
after she had given Mrs. Mallery some good advice
on the training of children, especially such untoward
children as her Tim.

By the next morning, whatever slight qualms of
conscience Reginald Beardsley may have felt on the
previous evening had quite given place to a feeling

of exultation that he had so completely succeeded
in deceiving his mother. He had intended, at first,
in case he was asked anything about the money, to
return it, and call it a good joke. He was surprised
to see the turn that affairs had taken. The temptation to keep the money became so strong when he saw
that his mother did not distrust him that the misguided boy readily yielded, and soon became so
hardened as actually to congratulate himself on his
"good luck," as he called it.

Early in the morning, Will Green, a chum of
Reginald's, and one of the most reckless boys in
Harrisburg, came into Mr. Beardsley's store to ask
Reginald to join him in a skating party the next night.
"Come on back here, Will, and we'll talk it over,"
called Reginald, adding in a lower voice, "Got just
the dandiest thing you ever heard of to tell you,—
just too rich to keep,"—he chuckled. By that time
they were snugly ensconced behind the great stove, well
out of the hearing of the other clerks; and Reginald
hastened to tell his little adventure about the missing
gold piece, forgetting in his excitement, that there
were other ears open besides Will Green's. Before he
realized it, his whispered conversation had given place

to an animated, though rather low, tone. Just as he was in the midst of the story, Tom Willis had occasion to go to the back part of the store to wait on a customer, when his attention was attracted by hearing his name.

"You see," Reginald was saying, "my pocket-money was getting rather low; and Tom keeps such sharp watch of things that I didn't see any way of getting more right away, but mother left just the amount I wanted on the dresser. It's Janet's money,—hired girl, you know,—but then, she's no good, doesn't half earn her wages, anyhow. Mother thinks little Tim Mallery's got it. She's going over there to make him own up—she'll scare him into it all right! —sh! there's Tom! Guess he didn't hear, though."

But all day long at school the guilty boy worried for fear Tom had heard something of what he had said; but after a little scheming and study, he made up his mind what he would do if he had heard, and should tell his father. It would take a pretty cunning falsehood to cover up his tracks; but poor Reginald was getting used to that. He felt sure, from past experience, that his mother would believe implicitly anything, whether reasonable or unreasonable, that he chose to tell her.

Tom Willis was sad beyond expression at what he had heard. He was sure that an innocent child was suffering reproach and blame that justly belonged to the unscrupulous son of his employer.

CHAPTER IX

OOR Tom was in a quandary. Mr. Beardsley had always been kind to him; but of late he had noticed a marked difference in Mrs. Beardsley's manner, which he rightly judged was because of his telling what he saw at Reddy's saloon. Should he inform Mr. Beardsley of what he had heard, and so run the risk of being discharged? He felt sure, for numerous reasons, that his employer's wife was not at all prepossessed in his favor; and he feared that if he did as his conscience dictated in the affair, the consequences might be grave for himself.

"I wouldn't care for myself, if it wasn't for Maggie—poor little sister!" he said to himself. "It would break her heart if I should lose my situation; but still she'd tell me to do right, anyway; she always does." So it turned out that before he went home that night, Tom had told his employer the conversation to which he had been an unwilling listener.

"I expected as much," said James Beardsley to himself, as he walked sadly homeward. "I must turn over a new leaf with that boy, or he is lost. But how am I to do it alone? I expect to have a hard task to convince Ellen that our boy is a thief. Father in heaven, help me!" he prayed.

Meantime Mrs. Beardsley prepared herself to call at Mrs. Mallery's lonely, tumble-down cottage. She felt that she must free her mind that very afternoon. It was stinging cold, and the sharp north wind sent the few stray flakes of snow whirling wildly about, as if they were trying to find a shelter from the pitiless blast. Somehow she almost wished she had not started out—almost wished she had been a little less positive. The old house looked so cheerless, so deserted, with its curtainless windows and its flapping clapboards, that the inmates naturally appealed to her pity. She drew her comfortable fur cloak a little closer about her. The blessed Spirit was pleading with her; and in spite of herself, Grandfather Beardsley's words about the charity which thinketh no evil kept ringing in her ears. Yes, she was really sorry she had started; but, seeing she had, of course it would never do to go back. Then she remembered that her husband had insinuated that Reginald had taken the money.

At once all her bitterness returned. She would prove to his entire satisfaction that their son would not stoop to such an act. Her hand was on the rattling door-latch—she had almost forgotten to knock. It had been years since Ellen Beardsley had called on

THE OLD HOUSE LOOKED SO CHEERLESS

her poor neighbor, and now to call on *such* an errand, —really, it did seem too bad! Mrs. Mallery heard the hand upon the door, and hastened to open it. A hollow cough greeted Mrs. Beardsley's ears as she entered.

"Indade, Mis' Beardsley, an' whativer sint the

loikes of ye over in the storm? Jump up, Timmie, and give Mis' Beardsley the sate.''

The rickety rocker which the pale-faced lad hastily vacated and respectfully handed to his mother's caller was the only chair in the room. Ellen Beardsley was actually ashamed, in presence of this kindly hospitality, to tell her errand; but pride and self-will prevailed. It was some time before little Tim could understand what was the trouble.

"What is it, mammy? what is it?'' he pleaded.

"Why, Timmie, don't ye understand? She thinks you're a thaif,—little Flossie's mother thinks *ye* stole her money.''

The big, hollow eyes seemed to grow larger, and the dark circle underneath them to grow darker.

"A dollar, mammy—a big round dollar—five of 'em? It's been a good while since I seen one.''

Again that hollow cough sounds out. Strange that Mrs. Beardsley had never noticed that the child was so slender and wasted. If it had not been for proving herself in the right, she would have gone home at once, satisfied of little Tim's innocence; but the stubborn fact remained that the money was gone. She knew Regie did not take it; Janet was gone that day; and of course Flossie did not have it, and baby could never have reached it. So Mrs. Beardsley resorted to new tactics. Reaching out her hand toward little Tim, she said: "Come here, child. Don't you see you *must* have taken it? There was no one else in the room, and I saw you near the dresser. I can't let Flossie play with you any more, unless you tell me the truth."

Then turning to Mrs. Mallery: "I don't want the money; you are quite welcome to that, but I want to know the truth."

Little Tim had seemed to hear nothing except the decree that he could not play with Flossie any more. Then he broke out into a loud wail: "O we was goin' to play Injun next time, and Flossie's goin' to show me her new pictures. I ain't got no money to give ye, but I want to play with little Flossie. *She's* good to me, she be."

The poor child seemed unable to understand anything more than that if he could only give Flossie's mother some money, she would allow him the privilege of playing with her little girl.

"W'en I git big, I'll earn a dollar, if I'm well, and *then* I'll give it to ye."

What could Mrs. Beardsley do? Mrs. Mallery sat upon the edge of the miserable bed, sobbing brokenly:

"An' to think of me poor little bye's bein' a thaif!"
Surely Ellen Beardsley's errand had been a success,
if her success might be measured by the misery she had
caused. But she was irritated. She didn't see why
Mrs. Mallery should "take on" so. Had she forgotten how bitterly she herself had resented the faint-
est suggestion that *her* son might have appropriated
the money? Ah, that was quite another matter!

There was but one thing left for her to do,—to
excuse herself to Mrs. Mallery and go home. Her
last view of the lonely house and its miserable inmates haunted her for days. It was of a wretched
woman, whose eyes were red with weeping, seated
in an old chair, clasping a hungry-looking boy to
her heart, and rocking back and forth in an aban-
don of grief and misery.

If Mrs. Beardsley was unprepared, even yet, fully
to believe in little Tim's innocence, she was still more
unprepared to hear her husband's explanation of the
miserable affair as he had heard it from Tom Willis.
She arrived home from her visit of "investigation,"
as she called it, in anything but a pleasant frame
of mind, and now to hear her husband's version of
the matter, and, above all, to see that he fully believed it, exasperated her beyond expression.

"I tell you, James, that Tom Willis is deliberately trying his best to ruin our son. I don't believe a word of his story—there."

"But, Ellen, you forget yourself. Do hear to reason; how could Tom have known anything about the affair, if he hadn't heard it from Reginald?"

"Well, I shall ask my boy, and I shall believe his explanation of it;" and the misguided woman left the room, weeping, not tears of sorrow over the wayward course of her son, but tears of indignation and anger.

CHAPTER X

REGINALD'S DUPLICITY

THE next half-hour found Mrs. Beardsley and Reginald closely closeted together in the lad's room. When they came out, Mrs. Beardsley's face was a puzzle; and as they passed Grandpa Beardsley's door, he heard her mutter: "I'll see about that Tom Willis; he has foiled me as long as I intend he shall. It is just as I told your father; Tom never can get over it because you took the prize in that spelling contest. You know he tried hard for it, and he's been determined to get you into disgrace ever since." If grandpa's blind eyes could have been opened, he would have seen such an expression of crafty deceit and cunning upon the lad's face as would have startled him. He had succeeded in deceiving his mother.

Whether it was on account of the nervous strain which Mrs. Beardsley had endured, or whatever may have been the cause, she awoke the next morning with a blinding headache.

Grandpa Beardsley was awakened by the sound of hurrying footsteps passing to and fro by his chamber door. Janet had returned the night before, and it was her steps as she hastened to the relief of her mistress, that had awakened the old deacon, who forthwith fell to musing.

"I wonder what Ellen meant by that remark I overheard as she passed the door last evening," he said to himself. "There's trouble brewing for that young man, Tom Willis, or I'm mistaken. He's a good fellow, and a Christian, I'm sure of that. I can tell one of the Master's sons from the tone of his voice and the words of his mouth. O, that the blessed religion of Jesus Christ prevailed in this unhappy household! Jimmie is trying to do what is right, but the poor boy gets no help from Ellen. Then there's Reginald!" and the old man sighed deeply; "he's no more like his father or his Uncle Paul than anything in the world. The more his folks do for him, the more he lords it over them with a high hand. There's nothing that boy wants but he gets it, and then he only asks the more. I don't believe his mother ever corrected him in his life, no matter what he did; and his father's getting so he's actually afraid to. Then the trouble his teachers have with him in school—it's too bad. I wish I could do something to help bring about a better state of things; but then, it's 'not by might, nor by power, but by My Spirit, saith the Lord.' But I can't help thinking of the difference between that boy and my Paul when he was his age. Why, he wouldn't any more have thought of giving me a disrespectful word than anything.

"I didn't do right by my children when they were little; I was too severe with them. Now Jimmie's folks are going to the other extreme, and that's just as bad," and the deacon sighed softly; "but God opened my eyes, and whereas I was blind, He made me see.

"How well I remember how pleased Paul was on his seventeenth birthday, when mother and Emma fixed his room all up for him—seems like yesterday! But I'm sure of this thing," he continued, "*all* children can not be dealt with alike. Some must be held in with bit and bridle; and some, well—just a word or a tear is enough for some. There's that baby Bessie, she's coming up in the same tracks as Reginald. I've seen Jimmie make some efforts to teach that child her place, but Ellen always blames him for it, and says she's too young to correct. Ah, me! things are not

as they were forty or fifty years ago. Well, the good
Book says that 'in the last days perilous times shall
come,' and that children will be disobedient to parents,
unthankful, unholy, and without natural affection. I
don't mean to complain, but the boy doesn't seem
to have a grain of common respect for me; Jimmie'll
see trouble with that boy. Maybe the good Lord will
let me lie in the grave before the worst comes," and
the old man sighed wearily.

Baby Bessie awoke early that morning, in her
worst mood; and as soon as breakfast was over, insisted upon going to mama's room. In vain Janet
protested, and explained that "poor mama's head
ached, and baby would make her worse;" she would
not be pacified, and her cries and screams resounded
throughout the house. "Me wants mama!" she cried.

"Dear me, baby, won't you go to Grandma?" persuaded Janet. "See! here is Bessie's nice, new dolly."

"Come and see sister, baby," called Flossie from
her chair.

It was of no use. Bessie seemed perfectly aware
that her will was being crossed, and that every one
was trying to pacify her, and this, of course, made
her determined not to be pacified.

"I can't do nothin' with the child; of course she

won't come to *me,*" complained Grandma Sharpe.

At this juncture Grandpa Beardsley offered his assistance as a kind of reenforcement, and the young rebel, still screaming lustily, was dropped into his arms. Smash! went the dear old gentleman's new goggles upon the floor, while his slippery little charge squirmed out of his arms in a moment, after inflicting an ugly scratch on the thin, white cheek.

At last, during a momentary lull, a faint voice was heard from the sick-room: "Bring her here, Janet."

There was a new chorus of howls while the transportation was being made, until finally the weary maid dropped her charge at the side of the mother's bed.

"Did they 'buse mother's darling?" A loud and long wail was her only answer.

"It's strange, Janet, that you can't manage to get along with that child. Why *don't* you learn to give her what she wants? You know as well as I do that she'll cry till she has her way. She always cries when her will is crossed, don't you darling?"

A chorus of shrieks is her reply, in the midst of which poor Janet beats a hasty retreat.

But now Mrs. Beardsley's troubles begin in earnest. The unreasoning child has caught sight of a toy whistle, unfortunately lying upon the bureau, and at once demands: ''Me wants whistle! me play toot-cars.''

In vain does the misguided mother, whose aching head has not at all been benefited by this course of treatment, protest that she can not reach the whistle. The naturally good memory of the child comes to her aid, and she remembers that mama said, ''Baby will always cry for what she wants until she gets it;'' so, nothing loath, she begins at once to act upon her foolish mother's instructions, with the result that the whistle is speedily forthcoming. Then she is ready to begin operations.

Trot, trot, trot, back and forth, back and forth, fly the little feet, to the shrill accompaniment of the whistle, until Mrs. Beardsley's worn-out nerves can endure it no longer, and she is forced to call Janet to the rescue; but it is not until every one in the house is entirely worn out that sleep comes to the weary little body—tired at last of being naughty— and quiet again reigns in the house.

I must now ask my readers to go back with me to the previous night, upon the evening of which Mrs. Beardsley and Reginald had their secret conference, when, as we must suppose, the scheming lad ''ex-

plained" how it was that Tom Willis happened to
know anything about the missing money. It seems terrible to think how it was possible for one so young to
conceive so much mischief, or to bring forth so many
falsehoods. But when one has once entered the school
of vice, it is astonishing to see how incredibly short
is the time required in which to be graduated.

The clock on the mantle has just struck the half-
hour past twelve; everybody is asleep in the house
except Reginald, and the flickering light thrown by
the street-lamp upon the walls of the lad's bedroom
remind him, in spite of himself, of Bunyan's "door
in the side of the hill," whence issued fire and smoke,
and which was the doorway to the pit. He has not
closed his eyes in sleep since his mother left the room.
He has a little errand to attend to, and he does not
care to be disturbed while attending to it.

The fire in the furnace still gives out a little heat,
but it is a bitterly cold night. Is it this that causes
the lad to shiver as he silently rises? Throwing a
large shawl hastily around him, he carefully opens his
bedroom door, and steps softly into the hall. Where
can he be going? See! he gropes his way along the
dark hall until he reaches the head of the stairs.

Half-way down the stairs, his foot presses upon a

loosely nailed board! What a loud creaking it makes! He never noticed that there was a creaking board on the stairs before. He is trembling in spite of all he can do. Ah! how true it is that guilt makes cowards of the bravest. We watch him with an interest that is growing more intense. Look! he is swiftly crossing the dining-room; the light from the street-lamp shows him plainer now. What can he want in the little room where the dresser stands? Listen! we hear a sharp clink, as of the ringing of a coin. The mystery is solved. The guilty lad has determined to return the stolen money, and persuade his mother that it has been there all the time; then Tom Willis, whom the reckless boy is beginning both to hate and to fear, will be discharged.

"Now," he whispers to himself, "I guess he'll not tell any more tales on me, and I've straightened little Tim Mallery's record out all right, besides; even father'll have to believe this evidence, and that pious chap will get his walking papers in a jiffy, or I'm mistaken. He's always preaching to me and croaking at me, and acts as if he couldn't rest till he tells father of every little thing I do. I don't care if he is poor, and his sister's sick. I hate him—*hate him.*

Ah, Reginald! would you tremble if I should tell

you that you are a murderer? I doubt not that you
would; and yet a greater than I has said it. The
mighty Judge, before whose face you must stand some
day, has pronounced you guilty: "Whosoever hateth
his brother is a murderer." There is no use in trying
to dodge the issue. Your own lips have condemned
you; and unless you haste with flying feet to the
"City of Refuge," the gates of that other city, whose
streets are gold-paved, will be closed to you. "For
without are .   .   . sorcerers, and .   .   . murder-
ers, .   .   . and whosoever loveth and maketh a lie."

As soon as Mrs. Beardsley had a few hours' quiet
sleep, she was able, though still pale and weak, to go
down-stairs. She determined to take Reginald's advice, and search more carefully in the place where
she thought she had laid the piece of gold, but she
did not expect to find it. She still believed that it
must be that little Tim had taken it; but in any case
she decided that Tom Willis must be discharged, for
hadn't Regie explained to her complete satisfaction,
how he had carelessly mentioned the affair of the lost
money in Tom's presence? Of course that was the way
he had found out about it, and had thereupon determined to cast the reproach of the sneaking theft
upon her boy.

Ellen Beardsley did not stop to think that the young man would not have had the remotest object in doing this,—so blind and unreasoning was her foolish prejudice,—so blind and unreasoning is prejudice always and ever. It matters not one whit where you find it,—whether in the church, wearing the garb of piety, or in the world hiding behind the mask of sincerity and the cloak of morality,—it is always the same. Prejudice thrives both in the church and in the world; and while Malice and Envy have slain their thousands, red-handed Prejudice has slain her tens of thousands. She counts her victims among the high and the low; and there is no sanctuary so sacred but she seeks to intrude her hateful presence, no soul so pure but her dark shadow at one time or another falls across the threshold of its most guarded portals. And wherever her shadow has fallen, there comes blackness and blight and mildew.

Ellen Beardsley carefully examines every place on the cover of the dresser where she might, in a fit of absent-mindedness, have dropped the coin. There are two or three little boxes,—no it is not in them,— wait! there it is now, in a little earthen cup, among odd buttons and marbles.

Her white cheek flushes and pales by turns. Little

Tim is surely innocent! Chagrin and embarrassment, anger and humiliation, rise in her proud, selfish heart, that her cruel folly and unjust suspicion should thus be made manifest. But great as is her chagrin, still greater is her secret satisfaction at being at last able to prove to her husband that his trusted clerk is guilty of telling a deliberate falsehood. He is a mean, sneaking fellow, in spite of his high profession and smooth words, and now she can prove him such. Mrs. Beardsley hastily takes the coin, and again seeks her own room, after asking Janet to tell Mr. Beardsley that she would like to see him at once, as soon as he came in.

"Well, Ellen," said Mr. Beardsley, opening the door of their room softly, "here I am; what is it, Ellen? a little better, I'm hoping," and he dropped into a chair, while his wife threw herself back upon the bed, and hid her face among the pillows.

James Beardsley could plainly see, from her excited manner and flushed face, that something unusual must have happened.

He was in doubt as to whether her communication would be pleasant or otherwise, and his curiosity was considerably heightened at the copious burst of tears which followed his question—for Ellen Beardsley had determined to be as impressive as possible. Hitherto she had failed in convincing her husband that it was for their interest, and more especially for the interest of their only son, that Tom Willis be discharged.

"Do tell me, Ellen; you're not worse, I hope."

"James, James, he is trying to ruin our son! I told you he was, but you wouldn't believe me; but now I have the proof. See here!" she cried, tragically dropping the yellow coin that had been the cause of so much misery, into her husband's hand.

"Whom are you talking about? not Tom? it can't be Tom you mean! Where did you get this money?"

"Where did I get it, indeed?—Just where I left it all the while; I was careless, I'll admit, and of course I was mistaken about Tim; but don't you see at last, that Tom Willis, the clerk whom you have trusted so long, and whom you think so faithful, is a hypocrite and a liar? Poor Regie was unfortunate enough to arouse his jealousy in that prize contest. Of course you can not be so unjust as to keep him in your employ any longer."

James Beardsley was perplexed. Already the correct solution of the mystery had flashed into his mind, with the certainty of conviction; but what could he do? He felt that he was powerless to stem the tide of his wife's prejudices, and he only replied: "I will dismiss

him, Ellen, though I am persuaded that it is most unjust; and what the poor fellow will do, with his invalid
sister on his hands, I can't tell;'' and James Beardsley
sighed heavily, and buried his face in his hands. He
was coming to see more and more, of late, the terrible
results of the unwise management of their children.
And now the words of the wise man rang in his ears
with a new meaning and a deep conviction of their
truth: ''A child left to himself bringeth his mother to
shame.'' Then he thought of the days of old, and
of Eli, the priest of Israel. What if a like terrible
punishment which the Lord brought upon Eli as a
result of the slack discipline of his sons should be
visited upon him?

But Ellen Beardsley had gained her point, and she
was contented; that is, as contented as an unregenerate
person can be. In her joy, she actually sent Janet
the next morning to tell Mrs. Mallery that the coin
had been found, and that she was glad to know that
her Tim was innocent; and also that she would give
her an extra day's work, with extra pay, if she would
come home with Janet. But what was Ellen Beardsley's dismay, a half-hour later, when Janet came
hurrying into the sitting-room, where her mistress
sat holding little Bessie, with the startling infor-

mation that she had found Mrs. Mallery sitting dejectedly by the bedside of little Tim, who was moaning and tossing in the wild delirium of fever. Mrs. Beardsley was conscience-stricken. Could it be that the child had been in the least affected by her foolish visit? And again the vision of the sobbing woman, holding a pale-faced boy close to her heart, and rocking back and forth in her cheerless room, rose in her memory; and with an anxious note in her voice, which she could not conceal, she asked: "What did Mrs. Mallery say, Janet? Tell me quickly —I must know. Did she say that I—that Tim—no, of course not; it can't be that the child cared anything about what I said that day! What did she say, Janet?"

"Well, now you've asked me, I suppose I might as well tell you that she *did* say that the child was almost sick the day you called, and he had been getting worse ever since. The poor thing didn't have hardly a brand of fire in the old stove,—said the wood and coal was all gone, but the 'poor bye wouldn't fale it if it *was* cold,' and she did not care for herself. It's too bad, Mrs. Beardsley! If I weren't a poor girl myself, I'd do something for her."

"Well, never mind, Janet," said Mrs. Beardsley,

coldly,—she could not endure the implied rebuke of her "help," though her own conscience, selfish as she was, was troubling her sadly,—"never mind telling me what *you'd* do. Just step over to the store and tell Mr. Beardsley to send over some coal to Mrs. Mallery, at once. But wait—did she say anything about the money?"

"O, yes; when I told her you had found it, she just broke right down and cried, and tried to make the sick boy understand, but she couldn't and then she cried and cried, and said—'too late.'"

"Dear me! I presume everybody'll think I'm to be blamed," whimpered the conscience-stricken woman, whose chief concern, however, seemed to be the fear that she should be censured. "Well, do hurry up, Janet, and have the coal ordered, and get back, and put up some food in a basket. I presume it will come good."

"You needn't send the coal, Mrs. Beardsley, for some of the other neighbors are ahead of you there. I saw a man drive up with some just as I left,—but I'll carry the food."

Janet did not return until a late hour that evening; and when she did, it was with the news that little Tim Mallery was dead. The doctor said that some additional trouble had set in, and the feeble,

Mrs. Beardsley had sat up, anxiously awaiting Janet's return. Somehow the memory of that afternoon's visit to her poor neighbor, and the little fellow's pathetic assertion that when he got big he would work and earn a dollar for her, if only he might play with Flossie, haunted her.

"Mrs. Mallery feels pretty hard toward you, I wouldn't wonder," remarked Janet, unable to resist the temptation to worry her mistress.

"Dear me, Janet, what did she say?" asked Mrs. Beardsley, irritably.

"O, not much! but the last thing the little boy tried to say—I heard him myself—was, 'I didn't take the money, mammy, tell 'er.' "

Ellen Beardsley could scarcely sleep that night; and when she did, visions of a thin, freckled face, and a pleading voice asking if he might only play with Flossie a little while, disturbed her slumbers. But instead of praying for divine grace, and for a new heart, which, like the Master's could be touched with the feeling of the infirmities and grief of others, Ellen Beardsley began to excuse herself, and to magnify her own virtues. Such is ever the manner of selfishness, and nothing but the refining influences of the Holy Spirit can uproot it from the human heart.

8

"Of course," Mrs. Beardsley remarked to Grandmother Sharpe the next morning, "I can't see how I am to be blamed for thinking the child took it; anybody would have said the same."

"But if you'd only heard to me," protested the old lady, "you wouldn't have lost the money. I told you not to take it from the woman,—she might have handed it to Janet herself another day,—but you never will hear to me," concluded grandmother, who seemed to think herself the oracle of the household, and to believe that all the miseries beneath the skies, especially those in her daughter's home, were caused by people's not "hearing" to her.

"I guess I'd go over, Ellen, seeing it's as 'tis," remarked Grandpa Beardsley, mildly. The deacon seldom ventured to make a suggestion of any kind, but he said this with a peculiar earnestness which irritated Mrs. Beardsley.

"Yes, I dare say you'd go over. I don't see what good I can do there. I've got something else to do besides running to the neighbors every time anything happens." Mrs. Beardsley had intended to go, but now she decides to ignore the whole miserable affair.

"Maybe grand'ther'd better skip over," remarked Reginald, sneeringly. "Say, grand'ther, don't you

think you might offer some consolation to the widow?
Better hop on my bicycle and ride over, and quote
some 'Scripture to the old woman, eh? come, you're
pretty good at quoting Bible; and that would give us
a little let up. We're getting tired hearing it, but I
dare say she'd like it;'' and with a rude laugh the
heartless lad left the room.

The old man sighed, and said earnestly: " 'Correct thy son, and he shall give thee rest; yea, he shall
give delight unto thy soul.' '' But his misguided
mother gave him not a word of reproof.

Of course poor Flossie was inconsolable when she
understood that little Tim was dead, and begged tearfully to be taken to see him. But Mrs. Beardsley
again allowed her pride and self-will to triumph over
every humane and kindly feeling; so Flossie had to
content herself with climbing into grandpa's arms,
begging him to tell her, over and over, what they
would do with Timmie, and if the angels would come
and get him some day.

"Will they put him in the ground, grandpa?''

"Yes, darling, in the ground,—the cold, cold
ground,'' repeated the old man, sadly. "There is
where they put mother, and Emma, and little Jennie.

Now don't cry, dear; let grandpa rock his little girl to sleep."

But Flossie was not to be comforted. To her loving child-heart a bitter affliction had come; and in her judgment a great calamity had befallen them. She looked out of the window at the huge drifting masses of snow, and the tears fell faster and faster, as she shuddered, and said wistfully, "Won't Timmie be awful cold, grandpa?"

"No, Flossie, child. Little Timmie will never be cold or hungry—will never suffer any more."

"When will the angels come to get him? O grandpa," and the tearful eyes brightened, "I just believe when they come after Timmie, maybe they'll take Flossie. Flossie's so tired."

"Yes, dear, when the angels come to get your little friend, we will all go, if we're good," answered the old man, wondering if the child's busy mother had ever taken time to instruct her little one in the blessed, simple truths of God's Book.

It would seem that this experience, sad and touching as it was, ought to have taken some of the inherent selfishness out of Mrs. Beardsley's heart. But after Tim's funeral, which she condescendingly attended, she seemed to forget all her resolutions to exercise more of the sweet charity which Grandpa Beardsley had suggested to her a few days before, and which he so constantly recommended by his own life. O, could her mortal eyes have scanned the book of the angel, as with unspeakable sadness he wrote the record of her life, she would have started back with cheeks white with horror. Mrs. Beardsley was a church-member, and actually believed herself an example of propriety in word and deed; but she would have seen on those pages, in letters of gleaming fire, "Weighed, and found wanting!" Still the tender Shepherd did not give her up. Selfish and unsympathetic as she had grown in years of prosperity, still she is the purchase of His precious blood. And as the refiner casts his pot of silver into the fire, and melts and remelts it, so the Great Refiner will not give her over until He has tested her in the furnace of affliction; until His great purifying fires have swept over her soul, and consumed the selfishness, and purged away the dross.

So may He never leave us, reader; so may He purify our souls, until we can cry from the depths of our hearts, "Search me, O God, and know my heart; try me, and know my thoughts; and see if there be any wicked way in me, and lead me in the way everlasting."

CHAPTER XI

———

TOM'S TRIALS

"I AM anxious to know if Mr. Beardsley did dismiss that good boy, Tom Willis," I hear somebody say. Certainly he did; for he had promised his wife to do so. But after the promise was made, James Beardsley felt very much as King Herod must have felt when, for his oath's sake, he beheaded John the Baptist in the lonely prison.

"I am sorry, Tom," said the merchant, the next Monday night after the promise had been made to his wife, "more sorry than I can express; but circumstances are such that—well—the fact is, my boy," he continued, with increasing embarrassment, "I must tell you "good-by' for good to-night. Something very painful has happened; but I hope you will believe that you have my fullest confidence, and very best wishes for success."

At the beginning of this little speech, Tom Willis dropped the scoop of sugar back into the barrel, in astonishment—he was waiting on the last customer before going home to supper—and looked up at the speaker with a pitiful attempt to smile.

"Yes, sir, I suppose—I think—I have rather been expecting it, sir," he stammered; "but still I had hoped it might not turn out so, after all. It is rather sudden, sir; but I thank you for your confidence in me. It would add very much to the bitterness of this night if I thought you distrusted me in the least."

"No, Tom, not a bit of it," said Mr. Beardsley, trying to speak cheerfully; "you have been a good boy ever since you've been with me—about five years, now, isn't it?"

"Yes, sir; ever since mother died. I've tried to be faithful and to make your interests mine, but——"

"Yes, Tom, I know you have; but the fact is, that missing money of the hired girl's turned up the other day, and the lad's mother thinks you told an untruth about him, and I can't persuade her differently."

"You are kind to try, sir, but you need not have done so; I am sure it is useless. But I trust God will make it all right some day, and I can wait."

"I presume you can get a job over at Mosely's

after a little. I heard he needed a clerk, and I'll speak a word for you."

"Thank you, sir," replied Tom. But it was with a sinking heart that he opened the little front gate that lonely night, wondering what Maggie would say —poor Maggie.

Tom had been brother, father, and mother—three in one—to his delicate sister, who was four years younger than he, ever since the death of their mother.

"Well, Tommie, hurry up! I've just outdone myself in generosity, and kept a nice piece of that shortcake you liked so well at dinner, in the warming oven for you,——why, what's the matter, Tommie? Something's happened. What is it, brother?"

"O, nothing, Maggie," replied Tom, feigning a carelessness, for his sister's sake, which he did not feel. "Nothing—only——" and then followed the whole miserable story.

"I was afraid of this when I told Mr. Beardsley," he explained. "But I could not endure to have little Tim Mallery bear the blame; and now that the poor child is dead, I should never have forgiven myself if I had refused to tell what I heard, and I knew you'd want me to do it; for you always say, just as mother used to, 'Do right, Tom, and never mind the consequences.' I'd have told you before, only I couldn't bear to worry you over what might never happen.''

The thin cheek of the slender-looking girl by his side grew white, but there was a brave ring in her voice as she answered: ''You did right, brother; I'm sure mother would have approved; I—I always test hard questions by that standard. You'll be sure to find work, Tommie. I know God will never let us suffer because you did what you thought right. Come now, while you eat your supper, let's talk it all over, and see if we can't make up our minds what can be done. Harrisburg is quite a large place, and I believe you'll find something to do, if we both only keep well,'' and she tenderly kissed the broad, white brow, from which the shadows were already retreating.

Before they slept, they had formulated their plans so nicely that they felt sure fortune would smile on them; and as Tom crept into bed that night, after saying his prayers, in which thanksgiving and gratitude had a large place, he felt far more hopeful than he had at first thought it possible to feel.

''Maggie's such an inspiration!'' he said to himself. ''God bless her. I hope she'll not get sick; but the dear girl is so slender. Somehow I feel as if every-

thing will turn out right. Still I wish I had a
little money saved up; but with Maggie's doctor
bills, and my small wages, it's been hard to save much.
I think Mr. Beardsley would have paid me more this
spring if I had stayed; but—it will be all right, I am
sure;'' which conclusion was but the natural product
of youthful spirits, good health, and a clear conscience.
But could the brave, young heart have felt that night
half the sorrows it was destined to feel before many
weeks, it would have been a sore trial to the faith
which now seemed so firm. But he was trusting in
God, and it is written that they who trust in Him shall
be as ''Mount Zion, which can never be removed, but
abideth forever.''

We will not attempt to follow our young hero
through the weary days of disappointment and weeks
of trial which ensued after his dismissal. More than
once he had almost regretted telling Mr. Beardsley
who had taken the servant-girl's money. What was
it to him anyway? Why need he to have cared so much,
even if the blame was laid on an innocent child, he
sometimes reasoned. Then He remembered that God's
Word was pledged that He would protect and care
for those who make Him their refuge; and his heart

would once more be filled with that sweet peace that passeth understanding.

The next day after leaving the employ of Mr. Beardsley, Tom visited the office of Mr. Mosely, as his late employer had suggested, only to find that the vacant place had been filled the week previous. Disappointed, though not discouraged, he called on many of his acquaintances, men who had always given him a kind word and a pleasant smile, hoping that some vacant place would offer itself. But poor Tom soon learned the lesson which is always so hard to learn, and which each must learn for himself, that it is one thing to find an apparent friend in days of prosperity, when the skies are sunny, and sweet flowers of hope and cheer are blooming in our path, and quite another to find that true friendship that is indeed "born for adversity," and which "loveth at all times." Indeed, he was quite at a loss to understand the averted looks and the cool answers that he so often received from some who had heretofore professed themselves his friends. But the mystery was clear enough "after many days," when he found that the cruel tongue of slander had not been silent, and that cunning falsehood had forged her subtle chain of hypocrisy and deceit, link after link, until every helpful avenue had been hedged up. For Reginald Beardsley had not been satisfied with the obnoxious clerk's dismissal, but he had been careful to set sundry mysterious stories afloat concerning him, and the reason of his leaving Mr. Beardsley's employ.

The weeks passed slowly by, and lengthened into months. Finally one afternoon in early spring, the pitiless tramp, tramp for employment had come to an end. The hand that the weary boy laid upon the latch of the little front gate, as he came home that evening, trembled with exhaustion, and the brow that his devoted sister tenderly and tearfully bathed was hot and burning with fever.

Mr. Beardsley had proved himself a friend all through the weary days, and had been the means of Tom's securing the little work he had found,—just enough to keep them from absolute want,—and Maggie's health had been much better than for a long time; so they were just beginning to hope that with the coming of spring, brighter days would be in store for them.

But now Tom threw himself upon his bed, and in utter loneliness and discouragement, gave way for the first time to bitter tears. What to him was the coming of beautiful spring? What to him were the songs of birds and the sweet-scented flowers? Weary, discouraged, and sick, a burden to his delicate sister, a burden to himself. Thus the weary days passed slowly away.

James Beardsley heard, with a sad heart, of his young friend's illness, and many little dainties found their way to the sick-room. But if he hoped that his wife's hard spirit would soften toward the young man, whom he felt sure she had deeply wronged, he was doomed to disappointment. Ellen Beardsley only shrugged her shoulders, and remarked that she didn't know as she was to be blamed because Tom Willis had been taken sick. She had considered him a deceitful, canting hypocrite—so she considered him still. And she had concluded her remarks by saying that she certainly did not think herself indebted to him after the manner in which he had treated her son.

So deceitful, so unfair, so unchristlike is selfishness. Woe to that human heart in which it takes up its abode. Woe to the life that is affected by its accursed influence. It palsies the hand of charity, and silences the tongue of kindness. It closes the eye of pity, and dries up the springs of tenderness and love in the heart where its baneful presence is found. Shall we cherish it?—you and I? Shall we bid it

welcome to our hearts? Shall we permit its blighting
shadow to fall across our paths to darken our own
lives, and to blast the lives of others? Or shall we
bid its hateful presence be gone, and so fill our hearts
with the sweet influence of the blessed Spirit, whose
fruits are love, joy, peace, long-suffering, gentleness,
and goodness, that there shall remain no room in
which the throne of selfishness can be set up, and no
foothold for its vile presence?

CHAPTER XII

WITH the coming of the sultry days of summer, it was evident to James Beardsley that his father was surely failing. No one else seemed to have the time or the inclination to note the trembling step, and the pale, worn face of the old man. When, indeed, he mentioned one morning that "father looked as if he had had a poor night of it," Grandmother Sharpe remarked quickly that *she* hadn't rested either, and she guessed other folks felt about as well as she did. It really seemed as if the poor old woman was cultivating the weeds in the garden of her heart, with more and greater success every day. Ah, how true it is that if we would make our gray hairs a crown of glory when age settles down upon us and throws its hoary mantle over us, we must see to it that we are found in the path of righteousness.

There was a wonderful contrast between these

aged people. The old deacon, with his kindly, dim eyes, and white hair, with his form bent, and his step tottering, had yet a voice as soft and gentle as a little child's, and a laugh as hearty as a boy's. A beautiful old man was he; for there is no beautifier

Grandmother Sharpe

like the peace of Christ. Grandmother Sharpe was tall, and straight as an arrow, and her gaunt figure seemed to grow more angular every day, and her voice to acquire an added degree of shrillness. There were two perpendicular lines between the straight brow,— lines plowed deep more by the fingers of ill-temper than by the hand of time,—which gave an additional fierceness to the small, deeply sunken, black eyes. Accustomed for years to speaking words of bitterness and jealousy, at last, perhaps as much from habit as anything else, they fell naturally from her lips, like

Grandpa Beardsley

sharp arrows, and, as the wise man says, like "a continual dropping in a very rainy day." The sweet language of kindness and love was to her an unknown tongue.

Ah, how many Grandmother Sharpes there are in

9

the world, and alas! in the church as well. Did you never meet one of them? Did you never form the acquaintance of one of these unhappy people? Let us be kind to them; for God knows they are to be pitied, but they are not all old women; indeed, there are some of them who are still young, but upon their brows little furrows have been plowed by another than the finger of time; for ill-temper is no respecter of persons; she writes her ugly autograph upon the brow of youth and the cheek of beauty. O, there are *so* many Grandmother Sharpes! Perhaps there is one living under your own roof, aye, more, it *may* be if you and I look closely into our own hearts, we may see her likeness there.

But, thank God, if there are Grandmother Sharpes, the world is not left without a few Grandpa Beardsleys in it. There are some upon whose shoulders the passing years rest lightly, and upon whose faces the finger of time leaves only a kindly imprint, whose silver hairs rest upon the noble head like a halo of glory, and through whose heart the peace of God flows like a river; whose saintly presence seems a benediction, and whose words, always fitly spoken, are indeed "like apples of gold in pictures of silver."

This is the sanctifying effect of years of "walking with God."

One sultry morning in August, Grandpa Beardsley did not get up to breakfast. Janet said he had called to her, as she was passing through the hall, that he was so weak he was afraid to try to go down-stairs. "If you will bring me a thin, brown slice of that nice toast of yours, Janet, I think I can eat it," he had said, in a voice *so* weak and altered that the girl was startled, and hastened to tell her mistress.

"Dear me," exclaimed Mrs. Beardsley, with an impatient frown. "Mercy knows I've got enough to do to-day, and enough for you to do, too, Janet, without bothering with him. It's queer just because the minister and his wife are coming to tea, and I've got this great ironing on my hands, that I have to be hindered just now. I declare it is positively annoying. I wish, James, you would go up and see if you can't get him down-stairs to breakfast. Tell him Janet has no time to fuss with making extra dishes," she continued carelessly.

Ellen Beardsley was not as heartless a woman as she seemed; but her better nature had become so warped by selfishness that she did not herself realize

how her cruel words rankled and burned in the heart
of her husband, who replied indignantly: "I shall tell
him nothing of the kind, Ellen; I intend that my
father shall receive attention when he is ill; if Janet
can not prepare him a slice of toast, I will do so
myself."

It was very seldom that James Beardsley expressed
himself so forcibly to his wife, and she was quite
stunned for the instant; after standing for a moment,
with brows elevated in astonishment, she called after
her husband as he was climbing the stairs: "Of course
Janet can make the toast; wait, Jimmie!" while she
added to herself: "I can't say the least little thing but
he's getting so he takes it so hard—I wonder what's
the matter with him."

What, indeed! ah, what will so gall and wear a
tender, loving heart, as the perpetual nagging, grum-
bling tones of those to whom we have given our love,
for whom we labor, for whom we sacrifice, and for
whom, indeed, we live!

"I'm so glad you came up, Jimmie!" exclaimed
the deacon, in a weak voice. "I've wanted to see you
alone for a long time," grasping the hand of his son,
and eagerly pulling him down to a seat on the bedside.

"What can I do for you, father? I hope you're

not suffering. We have another sultry day before us.''

"Suffering? O, no,—just weak, so weak; but you know, Jimmie, I've lived out my threescore years and ten long ago; and by reason of strength I have even gone beyond the fourscore,—but I'm getting to feel that my strength is labor and sorrow.''

"I can't bear to hear it, father; see, Janet has brought your breakfast; you'll feel stronger when you've eaten.''

"I was going to say to you, my son,'' continued the old man when they were again alone "that I am sure I shall not be with you long. Don't be sad; 'tis better so. I am only sorry that I have been so nearly helpless for so long, and that I have caused Ellen worry and trouble by my blindness. But old age will come, Jimmie; it will come.''

"I am sorry that our home has not been a more congenial place for you, father; I have felt this for a long time, but I seem to be powerless.''

"I know how it is, Jimmie; you have done your best to make it agreeable for me; but, O my son, I may never have another opportunity of talking to you. My heart acted strangely all night, and I feel that the end is near; but I should not die easy if I did not entreat you to lose no time in erecting the family altar—the altar of the Lord, which has so long been broken down.''

By this time the strong man was weeping silently; the gentle, melting Spirit of the Lord was softening his heart.

''I remember the time when I was converted all over again—mother and I. You and Jennie were young then, but I dare say you remember it. I wasn't doing right in my family; and now you're not doing right in yours. O my son, do let the Master make you all over again. He'll make it easy for you to serve Him. He'll carry you and your burden, too,—and—and you've got a heavy one, Jimmie. Yes,'' he continued, prophetically, the boy, Reginald, will give you much trouble; but God is mighty, and I trust the end will be peace.'' Then clasping the thin hands reverently, and raising the dim eyes to heaven, the soft, trembling voice slowly repeated: '' 'Thou shalt guide me with Thy counsel, and afterward receive me to glory. Whom have I in heaven but Thee? and there is none upon earth that I desire besides Thee. My flesh and my heart faileth; but God is the strength of my heart, and my portion forever.' ''

''God bless you, father; and God give you rest!'' said James Beardsley, earnestly. ''Your talk has done me good, but I would better go now. I fear you are tiring yourself.''

''Wait a little; not yet—don't leave me yet. I must have you a little longer by me, Jimmie. I am thinking of Paul. I wish you would get his last letter —it is there on the table—and read it to me once more. Paul and Jimmie, Paul and Jimmie,'' repeated the old man, tenderly, ''that's all I've got left now.''

With trembling voice the letter was read from the loved and absent son and brother, long a soldier of the cross in far-distant India. The old deacon listened eagerly. These were the closing words: ''Father's an old man, brother; and I greatly fear I shall not see him again in this life. I feel that you are specially blessed in having him with you; his presence is a continual benediction. But don't forget, Jimmie, you'll not have him with you long. But the King is coming by and by, and we'll all meet pretty soon— my brother, my dear, dear father, and mother, and Emma, and brown-eyed Jennie, if we're only faithful over a few things.''

''That sounds good, Jimmie; O that sounds good! Now you may go, but promise me first, Jimmie, that you'll not forget about the family altar when I'm gone—and—about Reginald. God will sustain you, my son,—but O, I entreat you, redeem the past as far as in you lies.''

"By God's help, father, I will try," was the trembling answer.

Just then a shrill voice came ringing up from the foot of the stairs: "Your breakfast is spoiling, James; do you forget that I am in a hurry?"

James Beardsley closed his lips to the indignant reply that almost forced itself from them. But when he saw the flushed, weary look on the face of his wife, as she bent over the hot stove, his only feeling was one of pity and love. Poor Ellen! Was this nervous, anxious, worried-looking woman, indeed the wife of his youth—the dear, spirited, brilliant girl that had won his heart? Ah, how many years ago it seemed—years full of the hurry and worry of life. How well he remembered when the baby came—a sweet, cunning, black-eyed fellow—little Reginald. How they had laughed over his cute baby pranks! How they had petted him, and coddled him, and fondled him! Alas, he saw it all now. That imperious will developed in early infancy had grown stronger every day, until it would not brook restraint. Then every year had brought new cares, new responsibilities, until the busy merchant had grown careless and worldly. God's

Word had been neglected, and the family altar had been broken down. Like Eli, he had not restrained his son, and now he must reap what he had sown. The lad had not returned home till long after midnight the previous night, and this conduct was getting to be so common as to excite no comment. At first he had remonstrated with the boy; but his mother could not endure that he be reproved or corrected any more for this than for his other bad habits, and always concluded every such effort on his part with, "Let the boy alone, James; you will drive him to destruction by your severity."

James Beardsley thought it all over, and, as never before, the Holy Spirit showed him his boy's danger, —aye, the Spirit opened his eyes to his own danger as well. He saw his godly and beloved father slipping away from him. O, that he had better heeded his instructions and warnings in the past! Now he resolved, in God's name, that he would live differently, —that he would redeem the past. And as his father had done on that Sabbath day so many years ago, but which was so well remembered as the beginning of a new life to them all, he, too, sought a secluded place, and there, on his knees, with streaming eyes turned toward heaven, the busy merchant, the man of cares, made a covenant with his God.

Grandpa Beardsley was so much better by noon that he felt able to come down-stairs for dinner. His daughter-in-law looked weary and dispirited, but a long line of nicely ironed clothes bore witness to her skill, and there was an array of luscious tarts and cakes and dainties on the shelves, waiting to tempt the appetite of the minister and his wife that afternoon.

Flossie's delight knew no bounds, because Grandpa was able to be up and dressed, though he was not strong enough to hold her in his arms.

After washing the dishes, Janet had undertaken the task of bathing and dressing baby Bessie. But as Bessie was uncommonly headstrong that particular afternoon, and had an unusual aversion to being bathed and combed, the minister, Elder Maynard, and his wife were announced before that tiny lady's toilet was made.

Mrs. Beardsley was particularly anxious for the child to "show off" well that afternoon, remembering that the minister had preached the previous Sabbath on the duty of parents toward their children. So she had been trying all the week to teach Bessie a few Bible stories, hoping to impress the minister as being a model mother. With what success we shall presently see.

As soon as the child heard voices in the parlor, she immediately decided that it was time for her to set out upon a tour of inspection and investigation; so, while Janet was busy preparing the bath for her, a half-dressed, begrimed, unkempt little object presented herself before the horrified mother and her amused guests, and before she could be prevented, had seized hold of the front breadth of Mrs. Maynard's delicate white dress with two dirty and sweaty little hands. In vain the embarrassed mother assured her wayward infant that the "bogy man" would catch her, and that Janet would "surely cut Bessie's ears off;" she could not be induced to relinquish her grasp of the dress, until the grimy little fingers were forced open, and she was dragged from the room, kicking and screaming: "Bessie *will* see the pitty lady! Bessie *won't* have nasty baf!" Mrs. Beardsley could have cried with shame and vexation.

As the angry screams resounded through the house, Grandpa Beardsley quietly remarked from his corner in the sitting-room: "A child left to himself bringeth his mother to shame."

It was some time before quietness was restored. But Mrs. Beardsley was determined to undo the bad impression Bessie had made; and so when at last, in a clean frock and shining curls, she again made her appearance, the foolish mother at once turned the conversation upon her: "Why! here comes mother's baby! how sweet her little curls look, don't they? Can mother's darling tell the lady who made her?"

"No, no!" screamed the little miss! "No, no!"

"What?" turning to the minister with a worried expression upon her face, "she can't have forgotten, can she?"

"I have no doubt she has," remarked that gentleman, soothingly.

"Of course, she is only a babe yet, but really she does know lots of things,—don't you, dear? Can't you count ten for the gentleman? come, do, now; there's a darling."

"One, two, sree!" announced the precocious infant, when she suddenly remembered that she was always accustomed to being "hired" to perform such unusual and astonishing feats.

"Candy!" demanded the shrill little voice.

"Yes, yes, dear; but count ten for the lady first. and *then* mama'll surely give Bessie her candy."

"No, no!" protested the child. "Me wants candy!"

"Janet!" called the indulgent mother, fearing a scene, "bring the dear child some candy. There, dear; *now* won't you count ten for mama?"

It did not take baby Bessie long to decide that she was being "shown off," and she determined to make the most of it. "Bessie *will* sing Dixie!" which announcement was followed by a shrill medley of unintelligible sounds which was surely "music" in nobody's ears but the delighted mother's.

"Now Bessie *will* play cars!" declared the inventive little genius, apparently determining to leave nothing undone on her part for the amusement of the guests. And, indeed, Mrs. Beardsley had seemingly no other resource at hand for the afternoon's entertainment, at least this was all that appeared to offer itself. Two or three times Mrs. Maynard had undertaken to introduce the subject of home missions; but this had proved to be only a futile attempt, being cut short by some unlooked-for antic from the child, to which, of course, prompt attention was at once called by the unwise mother. After a time, however, Elder Maynard, determining not to be baffled, again ventured a remark concerning the needs of the Mas-

ter's cause in far-away India, hoping that as Sister
Beardsley's brother-in-law was laboring in that field,
perhaps he could engage her attention. Vain hope!
Her only reply was, "Certainly," with an absent look;
and then she hastily added: "Janet, do put a clean bib
on the dear child. See how she has soiled this with
her candy."

All this time Flossie was arranging her pieces
quietly in her little chair, and troubling no one.

At the supper table Bessie was still the theme of
her mother's conversation, and it was with a sigh of
genuine relief that Elder Maynard and his wife
concluded their afternoon's visit, and bade their host
and hostess good night.

Reginald had not come in to his supper, his fond
mother having been unable to induce him to do so,
as he declared he didn't want to see the preacher.

After the guests had departed, Grandpa Beardsley's feeble voice was heard at the head of the stairs:
"Reginald, would you mind coming up to my room
awhile; I'd like to have a little talk with you?"

"I don't see what you want, grand'ther. I
haven't had my supper yet,—want to preach to me,
most likely. I don't care to hear it; I hear enough
of that down-stairs."

Ah, my boy, you will live to regret those cruel words; but bitter tears can never undo the past.

With a quiet sigh, that was almost a sob, the trembling voice continued, "Good night, little Flossie, I guess grandpa'll go to bed now."

James Beardsley had heard Reginald's cruel words, and a throb of anguish unspeakable thrilled his heart. "My son," he said, in a voice quivering with emotion, "I trust I shall never hear you speak to your grandfather again in so unmanly and disrespectful a manner."

"I don't know as I can blame him, James," hastily replied Mrs. Beardsley; "of course he doesn't like to be preached to all the while."

In humiliation too deep for expression, her husband listened to her reply, while a feeling surged over him not unlike that which one has who finds himself caught in a current too strong for him, from which, struggle as he may, he can not extricate himself.

An hour later James Beardsley stepped up-stairs, and opened the door of his father's room. The old man sat facing the large west window, in his old-fashioned, high-backed rocker. The setting sun threw a halo of light around the snowy head, and a solemn, sacred hush pervaded the room. What is it that causes the strong man's heart to grow faint, and his limbs to tremble as with palsy?

"Father!" There was no reply. The thin face is a trifle paler than usual, but a smile of infinite peace has settled upon it. The dear hands are clasped as if in prayer. Hush! break not the sacred stillness. Grandpa Beardsley sleeps the peaceful sleep that knows no waking till Gabriel's trump shall rend the dusty tombs, and the "dead in Christ shall rise."

James Beardsley buried his dead, with many tears, in the old cemetery at Jonesville, close beside mother and "little Jennie."

> Ah, there is no time when the human heart
>   So gropes in the gloom of night,
> As the time when we turn from our dead apart,
>   And cover them up from sight.
>
> And there is no time when our hearts so call
>   For the deathless home above.
> As the day when the clods of the valley fall
>   O'er the grave of the one we love.

"FATHER!" THERE IS NO REPLY

CHAPTER XIII

TOM AND MAGGIE

KIND reader, come with me to the little home of Tom Willis and his sister. It is a beautiful day in late September,—one of those delicious, dreamy days when it seems happiness unspeakable just to live. The air is laden with sunshine, and the gorgeous leaves of the old maples by the front gate quiver and tremble in the soft breeze, as if for very joy.

The front door of the little cottage is open, and a fair young girl is sitting by the window. There are traces of tears on her pale cheeks, and her eyes are dim with weeping. Steps sound on the gravel walk. Some one is coming through the gate.

"O Tom, is that you? The grocer sent his bill over, and it's a little higher than I expected. But see! I'm cheering up already, Tom;" and she smiled; a pitiful little smile it was. "Any good news, brother?"

"Well, Maggie, I got a few hours' work this afternoon over at Tupper's grocery doing some boxing; I brought you this basket of peaches,—beauties, aren't they?" said Tom, displaying the tiny basket of choice fruit, for which he had just paid his last quarter, hoping to tempt his sister's appetite with the unaccustomed dainty.

"O Tom, how good of you! but really, brother, we can't afford peaches. Just think, *peaches!* we haven't had one this year! Well, I'll banish the blues, and we'll have one good meal anyway."

"That's a dear little sister! Do you know, Maggie, I'm afraid we have been distrusting God for a while back! We've been so gloomy."

"Yes, Tom, but what are we going to do? The last dollar of our savings was gone last week, and your doctor's bill isn't half paid yet; and the grocery bill is due, and the rent,—and really, Tom, your old coat is getting to look too shabby to wear to church."

"Yes, Maggie, but God knows all about it as well as we do; He says He does. It's a great comfort to me to read, 'For your heavenly Father knoweth that ye have need of all these things.' We're trying to do right—you and I—and I feel more than I ever

A Fair Young Girl Is Sitting by the Window

did in my life, Maggie, that God will and does hear our prayers. And, even if we are destitute, it is not at all pleasing to Him for us to distrust His kindness or His care.

"By the way, I saw Reginald Beardsley to-day. He was hanging around Reddy's saloon with Will Green and Harry Coleman. O, if I could only do something to save him!"

"O Tom! I believe you'll be a missionary yet. I declare you make me ashamed of my own selfishness. Do you know, sometimes when I think how much that boy has done to cause us trouble, I just feel wicked, —I do, Tom, I truly do,—and here you're longing to do something to help him."

"Well, never mind, little sister; you'd be as willing to help him as anybody if you saw him in trouble. Let me tell you what I've been thinking for a long time. I've about decided to write to Uncle Ben, out in Dakota; you know he keeps a small grocery, and I've been wondering if he wouldn't give me a job. Of course, he's poor, and I wouldn't get very high wages, but it would be better than nothing."

"O Tom! leave me and go away out there! Away out to Dakota? O Tom!"

"I know, Maggie, but you could come after a

while. I hate to leave you, but maybe you might stay with Mrs. Hill till I could send for you. I don't feel very strong, someway, since that fever last spring, and it tires me more than I can tell you to run all around town after stray jobs, and then not get enough to do to earn half what you and I need to eat.''

''I know it, Tom; maybe it would be best; but I can't help thinking about Aunt Linda. I don't see what good she thinks all her money will do her by and by—she can't take it with her to the grave. O brother! if only the Lord would open Aunt Linda's heart.''

No wonder Maggie thought about Aunt Linda. She was her mother's only sister. Rich and prosperous, she had given small thought to her dead sister's struggling son and daughter, from whom she had scarcely heard in years. There had been a bitter quarrel when Mrs. Willis had married the handsome young man who inherited little from his father save a legacy of debt and a thirst for strong drink, which the poor fellow feebly fought at first, only to yield passively before many months.

It is not at all to be wondered at that Maggie often thought, during those days of darkness, of her aunt, and wondered vaguely why Aunt Linda could not be converted.

Listen, Maggie, listen to the words of the tender Shepherd of Israel; He is speaking to you even as He did to the faithless, trembling disciple of old: "O thou of little faith, wherefore didst thou doubt?"

Yes, my reader, he is speaking to you and me in tones of tenderness and love. Is the way dark? Does it seem that heaven is a long way off? Do you feel that you are in immediate need of help? Have you reached some crisis in your life, where it seems as impossible to go forward as it did to the trembling hosts of Israel—mountains on either side, the black waters before, the cruel enemy behind? "Go forward!" thunders the great Captain. But even as you go, behold the waters fall back; the clouds are lifted; light shines. "When thou passest through the waters, I will be with thee; and through the rivers, they shall not overflow thee; when thou walkest through the fire, thou shalt not be burned; neither shall the flame kindle upon thee."

It was finally decided that the letter should be written to Uncle Ben; though when the brother and sister bowed that evening in prayer, Maggie's thoughts

would, somehow, turn to Aunt Linda. At last she
fell asleep, with the words Tom had read from his
Bible ringing in her ears: "Fear ye not, therefore,
ye are of more value than many sparrows."

CHAPTER XIV

AUNT LINDA'S LETTER

OM sat at his little desk the next morning, pen, ink, and paper beside him. He was just beginning a letter to Uncle Ben.

"O Tom!" interrupted his sister; "I had such a happy dream last night; I thought I was trying to cross a deep river in a little boat. The river seemed so wild; and the waves, higher than my head, were just ready to come down upon me. I thought I could never reach the other shore, when there seemed to stand by me a beautiful woman, with wings of light. I thought she took her seat in my boat, smiled lovingly upon me, and with three or four strokes of her oar, landed me safely on the other side."

"Why, Maggie, it does a fellow good to hear that. It makes me think of the time Christ came and joined Himself to the disciples' boat in the midst of the tempest, and immediately it was at the land."

"Yes, but see, Tom; I didn't finish telling you.

Isn't it queer? I dreamed that as soon as I was safe on the shore, lo and behold, the lovely woman with the white wings was Aunt Linda. When I went to thank her, I awoke."

"That's a very good dream, little sister; now dear, keep real still, so I can finish my letter. Wait, there comes the postman. Just step to the gate, will you, and get the paper?"

"Tom Willis, see here!" exclaimed Maggie, hurrying up the steps, with more eagerness and enthusiasm in her manner than her brother had seen for many months. "Look quick! I just do believe we've got a letter from Aunt Linda! Anyway, it's postmarked 'Miles Creek.' "

"I declare, you're right, I do believe. Hurry up, Maggie! How you tremble! There! you'd better let me read it for you." And this is what Tom read:

My Dear Niece and Nephew: I can imagine your surprise as you open this letter. Wonderful are the ways of the Lord. All things are possible with Him. Perhaps you were too young to remember the story of the foolish quarrel between your mother and me. I shall not need to repeat it. But God has opened my eyes, and I can only praise Him. Three months ago the little boy died,—I always think of him as a little boy, though he was nearly fifteen,—whom we adopted when he was but a baby, and who was to us as our own son. Now the great house seems so empty! I have been wondering if you—Maggie and Tom—would be content to come and live with Uncle Walter and me, and help make our home peaceful and happy. I remember you both before your dear mother died. But in my blind selfishness, I did not love and care for the lonely children of my poor sister as I should. I must tell you that your Uncle Walter is anxious for you to take this offer kindly; and as Tom has had some experience as a clerk, I am sure he can make himself useful to his uncle. I hope you will forgive my past selfishness, even as I believe God has, and write very soon to your affectionate—

AUNT LINDA.

Tom was the first to speak, after the letter had been read. Maggie was silently weeping. "Well, little girl," he said, with a suspicious huskiness in his voice, "when do you think you and I will learn to trust? Providential, *isn't* it, sister? Now I guess I'll write to Aunt Linda instead of to Uncle Ben. Didn't I tell you, Maggie, we were doing wrong to worry so?"

"O Tom! to think that we can go together, and need not be separated after all! You can't think how I dreaded it,—and, besides, maybe Uncle Ben wouldn't have needed you. This is better even than to have kept on working for Mr. Beardsley. O Tom!"

Better? Yes. The Lord's ways are always better than ours—so much better. He is able to do exceeding abundantly above all that we ask or even think. And yet, like Tom and Maggie, we sometimes forget whose are the almighty Hands that are holding the reins, and guiding us onward over the uneven path of life, with more than an earthly father's tender care and solicitude. Then when affairs all at once shape themselves wondrously, and we are delivered from some sorrow which has threatened to overwhelm us, some trouble which has seemed ready to swallow us up, we remember that there is a God in Israel, and in shame and humiliation of heart we lay our hand upon our lips, in silence over our unbelief.

So it came to pass that one dull, cloudy day in October, less than a month after the receipt of Aunt Linda's letter, Tom Willis and his sister found themselves in the station at Harrisburg, waiting for the train which was to carry them to their new home in the sunny South.

The last few months had been sad ones indeed to them; but they could look back now and see the Love that had led them and the Hand that had guided them. Yet, when they had stepped out of the little front gate, and latched it behind them for the last time, a feeling of sadness unspeakable rushed over them. They had bidden good-by to each familiar room; the sunny front chamber, where their mother had died, always seemed associated with tender memories—memories which were darkened only by the picture of that terrible night when their father, mad with the delirium of strong drink, had breathed out his life upon the couch in the corner.

Mr. Beardsley had stepped down to the station to see them off; he had never lost his kindly interest in them.

"So you are off for good, Tom! God bless you! I hope you'll do well,—and—and you will. You have trusted in God, and He will never forsake you." Then he spoke of Reginald, and of his fears for him, and the sorrow of heart his wayward son had already caused him. "Father talked to me about my boy before he died; but he said the Lord was mighty, and he trusted that the end would be peace."

"I trust it will. We will hope for the best," Tom had answered, as he took his old employer's hand in a warm grasp and bade him good-by.

One by one the last familiar objects, the last well-remembered landmarks, had been passed. Already it was getting dark, and they could see the lights twinkling in the little stations as they whirled rapidly past. Grateful tears were shining in Maggie's eyes as she pressed her brother's hand, and whispered, softly, "Even the night shall be light about me."

> The darkness shineth as the light;
> The day is even as the night
> To Him who guides, upholds, protects,
> Who all my ways in love directs.

* * * * * * * *

James Beardsley sadly missed the gentle presence of his departed father; the example of a godly life never ceases, never dies. Like the gleaming stars of heaven, the influence of the just shines on and on, one generation after another. A passing cloud may seemingly obscure the light for a little time; but when the cloud passes, the tiny point of light gleams on, none the less brightly for the passing shadow.

And so, after the sudden death of the old deacon, the godly life which he had lived in so quiet and unostentatious a manner shone forth with added brilliancy. Even Grandmother Sharpe declared that a good man had passed away; and that she always *had* thought that if ever there was a saint of the Lord, it was Deacon Beardsley. Forgetful of the fact that the old man had ever aroused her envy and unreasoning jealousy, she spoke of him after his death only in language of praise!

Well, it is always so. Grandmother Sharpe was not alone in this peculiarity. It is human nature. Strange that while our dear ones are with us we are too often keenly alive to their faults, while we are blind to their virtues. But when the hand which in life we refused to take, or were too busy to hold in the warm clasp of brotherly love and friendship, is cold in death, and the timid feet, whose every stumble in life we were so quick to notice and censure, no longer climb life's hill by our side,—then we awake, as out of sleep, to see our mistake; and as if we could make amends for our neglect, we seek, like Grandmother Sharpe, to raise by our kindly words a monument for the departed.

The old man's heart had been so full of God's Word that it fell from his lips as the natural language of his soul. Sometimes a verse of Scripture would be the only answer he would make to a question; many times it was all the answer needed. But often, especially to Reginald, these apt replies had been only irritating and exasperating. But already the careless boy regrets the bitter, thoughtless words

11

he gave the patient old man on that last evening,—
the last words he ever spoke to him. He even wonders what his grandfather had wanted to say to him
that night when he asked him to come to his room.
The old man's pleading words ring in his ears with
strange persistency. He can not silence their echo.
If he gives an unkind, disrespectful word to his father, memory brings back at once the soft, tremulous
voice now silent forever, with its inspired words of
reproof:

"The eye that mocketh at his father, and de-
spiseth to obey his mother, the ravens of the valley
shall pluck it out, and the young eagles shall eat
it." Whenever he falls under the influence of bad
companions, he never gives heed to their evil advice,
but under the continual protest of that gentle voice
forever ringing in his ear: "My son, if sinners
entice thee, consent thou not," the rude lad, who
had always objected to being "preached at," was
forced to listen to many and many a sermon engraved
deeply upon his heart, long after the kindly voice
of the "old preacher" was silent.

Mothers, do you feel discouraged because your

wayward son heeds not your tears and prayers?
Teachers, are you about ready to give up the bat-
tle because your pupils will not heed your words—
the words of God? Hear Him speak, faithless one:
"For as the rain cometh down, and the snow from
heaven, and returneth not thither, but watereth the
earth, and maketh it bring forth and bud, that it
may give seed to the sower, and bread to the eater;
so shall My word be that goeth forth out of My
mouth; it shall not return unto Me void, but it shall
accomplish that which I please, and it shall prosper
in the thing whereto I sent it." The oath of the
Eternal is pledged; shall we believe it? It is the
will of the All-father that the gentle voice of His
aged servant shall ever "cry aloud," and "spare
not," even though the years may come and go. Like
the gentle Shepherd who left the ninety and nine,
and sought the one lost sheep until He found it, so
the influence of those precious words of God, repeated
so often by His servant, will faithfully and per-
sistently pursue the wayward youth over the mountains of sin and the dark deserts of unbelief, until
the angels around the throne shall echo the glad

song: "This my son was dead, and is alive again; he was lost, and is found."

> Ah, the Word of God! it is never lost;
>   It is clean and white and pure;
> O, bid it welcome within thy heart,
> It will cleanse the temple, and ne'er depart;
>   For the Word of God is sure.

There was one childish heart whose grief over the departure of grandpa was deep and sincere. Flossie was not to be comforted. Especially did she miss him when the little limbs grew weary, and the tired eyelids drooped; for at such times it was that grandpa used to take the slender little form in his arms, and in his peculiarly gentle voice, tell her his sweetest stories. And grandpa's stories had always served as panaceas when everything else failed to soothe and comfort the afflicted child.

With each succeeding day, it becomes more and more apparent to James Beardsley that he is fast losing what little influence he has ever had over his son. With a sinking at his heart, he notices the ever-increasing evil effect of bad companions upon him. The lad's mother still seems to be completely blind, not only to his faults, but also to his danger.

"When he is older, James, he will be all right. Of course, he likes young company; you mustn't think you can put an old head on young shoulders." With such arguments as these, Ellen Beardsley would seek to quiet her own and her husband's conscience.

CHAPTER XV

ONE evening before going to the store, and after praying to God for strength and grace to do his duty, Mr. Beardsley asked Reginald to step into the library for a few minutes' talk. The lad had been out until very late the evening before, and his father had decided that something must be done.

"I don't care to talk with you; I am just going over to Harry Coleman's. Will Green is at the gate now, waiting for me."

"Never mind, my son," said his father, firmly, "I will tell him he need not wait; he can go alone as well,—or I will invite him in."

While his father stepped to the hall door, Reginald turned an appealing look toward his mother; but at that moment she had left the room. There was no alternative; he knew that Will Green would not come into the house at his father's invitation. With an angry flush mantling his cheek, he stepped

166

into the library, and took a seat as far as possible from his father's chair.

"Come nearer, Reginald, we are only going to have a little talk; that's all." The father's voice trembled with earnestness as he continued: "I am sure I have never done my duty by you, Reginald. I have failed in not making myself more of a companion for you, and I am sure I have made a mistake all along. I have not brought up my children in the wisdom and fear of God. There is not a day that I do not regret the past more than I can express; and I know that I am only doing a duty that should have been done long ago, when I tell you now that I must insist that you quit the company of bad boys upon the streets, and come home evenings at a reasonable hour."

" 'Reasonable hour'!" sneered the lad, his voice trembling with passion. "Seems to me I'm getting old enough to be my own judge as to what company I shall keep."

"O Reginald!" pleaded his father; "don't you understand? I am older than you; and you surely should be willing to abide by my judgment, when I have only the tenderest feelings of love in my heart for you. You are quite welcome to bring any of your companions here whenever you like. You have a cozy room, and I am sure your mother and I will try, and do try, to make your home a pleasant one for you. My dear boy, why will you choose the streets? You have your books and piano; I am sorry these things are getting to be distasteful to you. We are trying to make your home *happy* for you, and O, how I wish you would try as earnestly to make your parents' home a *peaceful* one. You are very dear to me, Reginald; I don't suppose you can understand the depths of a father's love.''

If the stubborn boy had looked into the tender face bent toward him so appealingly at that moment, he would have seen tears of affection and love upon the cheek pale with emotion. But he had so long been accustomed to having his own way, that the seeds of selfishness had already taken firm root in his heart, and he had no notion of being ''domineered over,'' as he called it. If he had even then heeded the still, small voice of conscience, faint though it was, he would have thrown his arms around his father's neck, and begged his forgiveness for causing those tears of grief. As it was, he only repeated his father's words, with a bitter sneer: '' 'A father's love'! Great evidence I've had of it to-night, I think!''

Ah, there was *one* evidence of love which had always been lacking in the management of James Beardsley's son.

"What is that?" you ask, in surprise. Reginald Beardsley has always been surrounded by everything necessary to his happiness. He has never known what it was to deny himself in ever so slight a degree for the benefit of others. His every whim has been gratified by an indulgent mother and an affectionate father. His home has been made pleasant, and his surroundings cheerful and attractive.

Well, what was the mistake that James Beardsley and his wife had made in bringing up their son? Perhaps the wise man, with the divine light of inspiration directing his pen, can tell us. Listen: "He that spareth his rod hateth his son; but he that loveth him chasteneth him betimes."

"O, but," I hear some one say, "we have outgrown such a heathenish doctrine as that; the world is too enlightened for such teaching."

Ah! there are many nowadays whose fancied wisdom is so much greater than that of Solomon, though his pen was guided by the almighty Spirit of Him

who is the great Source of all wisdom, that much
I fear I shall bring upon myself the criticism of
some sage of this nineteenth century for being so
bold as to repeat such texts as these. However, I am
sure Solomon would not have approved of making
use of ''the rod'' except in love, and in that same
wisdom that inspired him to write these words.

Just then Mrs. Beardsley came into the room.
''What is the trouble, James?'' she asked.

Before Mr. Beardsley could answer, Reginald exclaimed, with the confident air of one sure of gaining
his case, ''O, he's chosen this evening to give me a
free lecture, because I was going over to see Harry
Coleman and Will Green.''

''Dear me, James! really, I'm getting tired of
acting the part of peacemaker. Why will you insist
upon preaching to the boy so much? I'm as anxious
for him to do right as you are,'' continued the unwise woman, ''but I don't believe in tormenting him
all the time. Do let him go, if he wants to.''

''Father in heaven, help me!'' exclaimed James
Beardsley, who felt as if it would perhaps have
been better to leave unsaid the words which were
so lightly esteemed. With a heavy heart he saw

Reginald—a gleam of exultation in his eyes—put on his cap, preparatory to going out into the street.

"Can't you see, James," continued Mrs. Beardsley, "that you are making a great fuss about nothing? I don't believe there's anything very bad about Will Green. His father is one of the wealthiest men in town, and a church-member. I'd hate to offend him."

"Yes, Ellen, but I've seen the young man worse for liquor a number of times," replied her husband, earnestly, while such a feeling of utter loneliness came over him as he had never felt before. Must he walk the long pathway of life alone? Must his dear wife ever be a stranger to the God he himself had so long slighted and neglected?

Ah, James Beardsley is not alone in his sorrow. Thousands all over the land share his loneliness. Husbands and wives walk the path of life together many a year, and are yet only strangers to each other,—one acquainted with the peace of God; the other an alien to the Father's house; the one cruising about on an unknown sea, without chart or compass; the other led on by angel hands.

Methinks that I stand by a deep, mighty river,
  That silently flows toward an infinite sea;
And sometimes its waves dash in pitiless grandeur,
  And sometimes it murmurs like music to me.
And look! there are barges with white banners streaming,
  So swiftly and silently passing along;
And the prayer of the saint and the curse of the scoffer,
  Are strangely commingled with reveler's song.
And some of the barks are enshrouded with darkness,
  And some wear a halo of heavenly light;
And some are led on by the hand of an angel,
  And some by the furious demons of night.
And some are in quiet, and some are in strife;
  Ah! this is a picture—a picture of life.

The evident lack of sympathy from his wife, and her complete blindness to the true state of affairs, together with his son's rebellious spirit, were a sore trial to James Beardsley. Then, too, it seemed that Grandmother Sharpe grew continually more querulous and jealous-hearted as the weeks went by. The contrast between her life and the beautiful and peaceful one which his godly father had lived seemed even greater than when Deacon Beardsley was with them. But all these things only gave him a clearer sense of his dependence upon God. Especially had he felt blessed in taking up the one duty which, above all

others, his beloved father had urged him not to neglect,—that of erecting the family altar, which so long
had been broken down. These seasons of Bible reading and family prayer, though seemingly only a
trouble to the older members of the family,—a mean-
ingless ceremony, to be hurried over morning and
evening,—were to little Flossie seasons of special delight; then she could hear her father read the beautiful stories of Joseph and Benjamin and David and
Samuel, with which Grandpa Beardsley used to be-
guile the tedious hours when she was so tired. Particularly did she enjoy the sweet story of Jacob's
dream of the angels; and that of the mountains that
were full of horses and chariots of fire round about
Elisha; and she always listened to the story of the
birth of the Christ-Child, and of the angels' song,
"On earth peace, good-will to men," with ever-
increasing interest. In fact, any story in which the
angels bore a prominent part was sure to be regarded
with favor by this "strange child," as every one
called her. It seemed as if the little heart was growing daily more patient and tender, and that these
lessons of divine truth were sinking deeper and deeper
into it.

Fathers, are you neglecting this means of grace

in your family? Are you more anxious to settle down
with the evening paper in your hands than to read
the message God has for you in His Book? Ah, why
do we welcome with such gladness letters from our
absent loved ones, while the grand old Letter from
heaven is neglected day after day? Children, you
have a message from the skies to-day—a message from
heaven directly to you. Have you read it, or have
you neglected reading the message of your best Friend,
which tells you He is coming again,—yes, and coming
soon,—and teaches you what you may do to get ready
to meet Him?

Little Flossie surprised everybody with whom she
came in contact—and none more than her wayward
brother, Reginald—by her quaint, womanly conduct,
and strange fancies. One day when her "big
brother," as she called him, was wilful and unkind,
Flossie looked at him pleadingly, and said, softly,
"Please don't, Regie; you hurt Flossie. See! the
angels are crying!" and the impulsive lad turned
suddenly, and giving the pale little cheek a kiss,
siezed his hat, and dashed out of the house, saying,
"O puss! you do make a fellow feel so mean!"

The death of little Tim, her never-to-be-forgotten
playmate, made an impression on the sensitive mind

of the child, which had never been effaced. Later, when her beloved grandfather died, it was the first time she had looked upon death; and for months she was so lonely and heart-broken that nothing less than "angel stories," as she called them, would comfort her. Her playmates—little Tim Mallery and Grandpa Beardsley—were gone; and, as if their places could never be filled again, she seemed to care less and less for the companionship of other children, playing her quaint little games either entirely alone, as she sat in her wheel chair, or with little Bessie. But Bessie generally soon wearied of Flossie's quiet plays and trotted off to find some noisier sport. At such times, perhaps because she more keenly missed her grandpa than at others, she loved to close her eyes tight, and wheel softly across the floor, back and forth, "playing blind," like poor grandpa.

* * * * * * * * *

It was the next week after the events recorded in the last chapter—a dismal, snowy afternoon. Great gusts of wind howled and moaned around the house, like the evil spirit in the parable, seeking rest and finding none.

Mrs. Beardsley and Janet were unusually busy, and Grandmother Sharpe had gone to make an afternoon call. Little Bessie had not been very well all day, and was asleep in her crib; and Flossie was quite lonely. She had played all her simple games, with an imaginary playfellow; had looked at the pictures, one by one, in her latest new book; and at last had taken her basket of calicoes, and spread the gaudily colored pieces down carefully, patting out every wrinkle with the delicate little hand again and again. At last a bright thought struck her,—she would ask mama to cut dolly a new frock from one of her largest pieces.

"Please, mama," she called, as she slowly wheeled her chair out into the kitchen, where Mrs. Beardsley was busy making cookies, "won't you cut dolly a nice new dress?"

At that moment Mrs. Beardsley was irritated— she had burned a large tin of cookies. For that simple reason, and that alone, she answered the child harshly, and with an impatient frown: "O, go away, Flossie, do! here I've burned all these cookies,—just ruined them,—and I'm in such a hurry!"

Mrs. Beardsley did not often speak unkindly to this little daughter whom she dearly loved; but we all understand well enough—aye, too well—by our own experience, how sometimes under very slight provocation, we speak unkind words, the memory of which

is afterward gall and bitterness because of some trifling circumstance that has irritated us, and caused us
to lose for the moment our self-control. O, those moments of thoughtlessness, those moments when we forget ourselves, and let go the hand of our good angel!
How many days and years of regret and sorrow of
heart they have cost!

Flossie was quite stunned for the moment; she
could hardly believe that her mother had been speaking to *her*. But she turned away sadly, with a little
ache in her heart, and, choking down a sob, wheeled
slowly back through the hall, saying to herself: "Mama's too busy; poor mama." Just then Mrs. Beardsley opened the trap-door in the kitchen floor, and
hastily went down cellar. She intended to be gone
only a moment, and knowing that Bessie was asleep,
and thinking Flossie had returned to the sitting-room,
she had no thought of fear from the open door. But,
failing to gain the attention of her mother, Flossie
had determined to fall back upon her old source of
amusement—"playing blind."

"I'll play I'm grandpa—blind—so—so; now I'll
walk"—she always called it "walking" when she
turned the wheels of her little chair. Then she begins
her journey back and forth through the hall; with

12

some difficulty she passes through the door of the kitchen. She had done the same thing—played the same way—many times before. The open trap-door is just in front, not a yard distant. Still Mrs. Beardsley tarries in the cellar, unmindful of the danger to her child. Slowly the small wheels revolve; the little chair pauses a second with its precious freight, as if dreading to make the fearful leap; and then it goes plunging downward.

THE WHEELS PAUSED A MOMENT AS IF DREADING
TO MAKE THE FEARFUL PLUNGE

CHAPTER XVI

ITH a cry of anguish and horror, Mrs. Beardsley rushed to the place where the limp form of her child lay.

"Thank God, she is alive!" she cried, as a feeble moan of pain fell on her ear. The child, at first stunned into unconsciousness, was in another moment keenly alive to her pain. But the fact that she was not dead filled the mother's heart with a deep gratitude, though she saw at once that one tiny arm was broken. "But she lives, thank God!" said Mr. Beardsley, when he reached home in response to a hasty summons. Ah, little Flossie! your mission is not yet accomplished. The angels of whom you so delight to hear, have been sent to preserve you.

"She will soon be all right again, Mrs. Beardsley," said Dr. Brown; "all she needs is quiet and good nursing for awhile. Young bones soon mend, and

181

the knitting work will soon be done," he smiled, with an attempt at humor.

But the days and nights seemed longer than ever to the afflicted child, and wore upon the delicate little form greatly.

Of course, Grandmother Sharpe did not forget to declare, earnestly and often, that the accident would never have occurred if *her* advice had been heeded. But this accident, sad and painful as it was, accomplished at least one good thing. Flossie never grew tired of telling her big brother how the "pretty angels" had saved her life; in fact, the child could not bear to have him out of her sight in the evening. So it came to pass that many an engagement with "the fellows" was broken off much to Reginald's chagrin; for he had not the heart, rude and boisterous as he was, to refuse to amuse his little sister. James Beardsley noticed with a thankful heart the unconscious modulation of his son's loud tones whenever he spoke to the gentle little sufferer, and the air of tenderness which fell upon him. Ah, love is mighty! it transforms the most rebellious heart; it makes sweet and pure the most obstinate spirit. It is the very name of God, and there is power in it. How earnestly the father hoped that Reginald's love for his little sister might yet prove to be the one tender spot in his rebellious heart.

After some weeks had passed, and Flossie was able to be out again in her little chair, one morning a letter came from Tom Willis, addressed to his old friend and employer.

James Beardsley was sitting with the family at the breakfast table when the letter came. He recognized the familiar handwriting at once, and knowing the bitter ill-will in the hearts of his wife and his son against the young man whom they had so wronged, he hesitated about opening the letter in their presence. Reginald's quick eye, however, detected his father's hesitation in a moment, and one glance at the envelope was enough to assure him that the letter was from Tom.

"Hello! got a letter from our 'pious friend,' have you?" questioned Reginald, with a sneer. "Strange, I never could be at peace with that chap, hard as I tried. I expect my exemplary conduct was such a reproof to him, he couldn't stand it," he continued, mockingly. "Well, maybe I'll turn out as well as he does, for all he's such a goody-goody," he added, bitterly.

"Your language pains me very much, Reginald.

I do not think Tom Willis ever did anything to injure you, and I think the day will come when it will be proved to the satisfaction of every one," said Mr. Beardsley, slowly unfolding the letter.

Ellen Beardsley's cheeks had begun to grow hot, and her eyes to flame, before her husband had finished speaking.

"I suppose you allude to me, James—I must be the 'every one' to whom you refer. I can't understand how you can possibly be such an unnatural father. It is plain to be seen that you prefer the son of a stranger—a poor, miserable drunkard—to your own son; and making such high professions as you do, James, I don't see how—really, I can't understand you."

"No, Ellen, I am sure you don't understand me. Would to God you did, and that we might both better understand our duty as parents before Him," said Mr. Beardsley, sadly.

"O, well, there is no use in talking about it; we shall not see at all alike on this subject. Would you care to read your friend's letter to your family, or is it such a treat to be reserved for more appreciative ears?" sarcastically rejoined Mrs. Beardsley.

It could easily be seen from whom Reginald inherited his cutting speech and imperious manners.

I am sure my young readers are anxious to hear from Tom Willis by this time; so we will listen as Mr. Beardsley unfolds his letter and begins to read:

MILES CREEK, March 14, 18—.

Mr. James Beardsley,
    Harrisburg, ———.

MY DEAR FRIEND: I am sure you will be glad to hear that my sister and I are very happy in our new home. We have found such friends as we never expected to find on earth. God has been good to us; and, after the dark and bitter experience which the last six months in Harrisburg brought us, the change from darkness to light, from bitter to sweet, seems all the more wonderful. Yet I can see that those lonely days of trial were not sent in vain; they were not purposeless. God had a sweet lesson for us to learn—a lesson of faith and trust—which I only wish had been better learned.

I thank you for all your kindness to me; and, let me add, I have the fullest confidence that some day it will be clearly proved to Mrs. Beardsley that I have never intended to wrong Reginald in the least. But I can wait the will of the Lord, who says that circumstances are brought about, not by might nor by power, but by His Spirit. Yes, as I said to you once before, I can wait.

Uncle is very kind to us, and I am helping him in his store, and attending evening school. Sister Maggie has improved very much in health and spirits. This warm southern climate appears to agree with her. Please remember us kindly to any who may inquire about us.

Very sincerely yours,
Tom Willis.

The next afternoon after the receipt of this letter, Reginald came home from school at an unusually early hour, and it did not take his partial, keen-eyed mother long to notice a peculiar nervousness and agitation in his manner. The fact was, he had at last been expelled from school.

"Why, Regie!" began his mother, with an anxious look at the clock, "how is it that you are home so early? You're not sick, I hope," she added, though something in the young man's appearance told her that it was an affair of far more serious nature than a trifling indisposition. Ellen Beardsley almost held her breath, awaiting his answer.

"Yes, I'm sick; fact is, I've been sick a long time —sick of school. Professor Hill is nothing but a crank anyway. I've learned all he knows how to teach me, and now I propose either to stay at home or else go out to Uncle Earl's to school. I'd like to graduate, and I don't see why I can't go."

Reginald knew well what wires to pull when he

wanted his own way. He had long tried to gain his parents' consent to going out to Uncle Earl's, his mother's brother, who had no children except one daughter. The boy could not endure even the little restraint put upon him at his home, and he longed to be free. Uncle Earl was rich; and Reginald fancied that if he could only live with him, he could do as he liked.

"What's happened, dear? You haven't been dismissed from school? Has Professor Hill,—after all we've done for him,—how I do despise an ingrate!" exclaimed Mrs. Beardsley.

Professor Hill was a poor man; and when he first came to Harrisburg, Mr. Beardsley had been the means of getting him a position as principal in one of the public schools, and had aided him financially. This Mrs. Beardsley never forgot; and though the perplexed teacher had done the best he could for Reginald, she always accused him of ingratitude when any trouble occurred with her son.

"Yes, he has; I've been expelled. That's the long and short of it. Maybe I'll get even with him yet, sometime!" exclaimed the misguided youth, whose chief desire had always been to "get even" with any one who, as he fancied, had done him a wrong.

It was this evil spirit of revenge that had prompted him to cause the dismissal of Tom Willis. Alas and alas that his unwise mother never had rebuked this indication of a cruel, revengeful disposition in her son, even as she did not now do! She only shrugged her shoulders uneasily, and said: "I don't care to have it get out, Reginald. I don't know what the Greens or the Willoughbys would say or think. Likely they wouldn't understand, and think it a great disgrace."

Ellen Beardsley did not even take the trouble to inquire into the nature of her son's difficulty at school. It did not occur to her that he could be in the wrong; but she was greatly distressed at the thought of his leaving home, and hoped to be able in some way to bring about a reconciliation with the teacher, so that Reginald need not bear the disgrace of expulsion.

But Professor Hill had already called to see Mr. Beardsley at his store, after school; so, when the latter came home to supper, and his wife proposed that he see the teacher and arrange some compromise, as he had often done before, she was met with the reply that it was useless. "I feel the disgrace of this miserable affair keenly," Mr. Beardsley explained, "but it is of no use. I said all I could to Professor Hill. He declares the boy to be completely beyond his control, and says he can no longer put up with the effect of his demoralizing conduct on the other boys."

" 'Demoralizing conduct,' indeed!" sneered Mrs. Beardsley. She was irritated at once by detecting an inclination on her husband's part to sympathize with Professor Hill against Reginald. "I suppose Regie is no worse in school, and causes no more trouble, if the truth were known, than Will Green, or Frank Willoughby, or any of the other boys; but the Greens and the Willoughbys are rich. O, it's the money, James,—it's the money,—I know; and," she continued, bitterly, "to think of how much you've done for that man!"

"Well," chimed in Grandmother Sharpe, the usual injured look very prominent in her face, "*I* told James not to help that schoolmaster, nor to lend him no money. *I* could see, well enough, how 'twould all turn out. He don't think no more of you, nor favor you no more, 'n if you'd never helped him. He's dretful ongrateful—a turnin' your only boy out of school! It's quare; nobody pays no heed to what *I* say."

"Professor Hill has done the best he could with Reginald, grandmother," explained Mr. Beardsley, mildly. Grandmother had always seemed unwilling to lend a helping hand to those in trouble, for fear they would not appreciate what she had done. There are many like her who let pass countless opportunities for doing good, from a selfish fear that their own vanity will not be pampered, and their virtues magnified, by the recipient of their favors. Have we not all met persons whose chief concern appeared to be, not to do good for the sake of helping and uplifting fallen humanity, but apparently that some one might owe them so overwhelming a debt of gratitude that every one would agree that it could never be paid. Then they pat themselves on the back, assume a wounded air, and declare that they are unappreciated, and that the world is very selfish and ungrateful.

"Well, James," continued Mrs. Beardsley, ignoring her mother's remark, "I don't know how *you* may look at it, but *I* am of the opinion that Regie would better finish his education and graduate, in spite of Professor Hill or anybody else. I don't propose to have the poor boy crushed and kept under, just because he happens to have a little more spirit

and pluck than the other boys. Nobody knows—
not even you, James"—whimpered the excited woman,
"how hard it would be for me to give my boy up,
even for a few months; but I can do it for his
good—I can do it."

"I presume you think it would help matters
to send him out to his Uncle Earl's. But you know,
Ellen——"

"Yes, I know—you're going to object. You always do if I set my heart on anything. I tell you
I want my son to graduate, and make his mark in
the world."

"I am as anxious as you are on that point, Ellen;
but you know, well enough, that Earl is not a Christian; and I would like our son to be under Christian
influence. Of course, Earl is eminently respectable
and all that, as far as the world goes; but I fear
for the influence on the boy. If he were only a
Christian——"

"O dear! you're so straight-laced, James. I've
no patience with you!" and Mrs. Beardsley turned
away, fretfully.

Reginald had been an unobserved listener to this
conversation; and now, snatching his cap, he hurried

out of the house, more determined than ever that he would overcome his father's scruples, and before the winter was over, be his own master, and enjoy perfect freedom at Uncle Earl's. Still the boy had moments of real sorrow over his own waywardness, and at last he determined to promise his father that he would certainly do better, and would quit the company of bad boys altogether, or else try to induce them to visit him at his own home. For a week after his promise was made, which he really intended to keep faithfully, the lad was so good and obedient that his father at last gave a reluctant consent to his going away to school; and the next Thursday afternoon was appointed for his departure.

But a whole week of orderly conduct, of respectful attention to his parents' wishes, of staying at home or helping his father at the store evenings, and going to bed when the other members of the family did; in short, a whole week of unreproachable conduct, seemed an age to the self-willed lad and was almost more than he could endure; so the reformation which his anxious father and too sanguine mother had hoped was to be permanent, proved, before the week was gone, to be of very short duration.

The evening before he was to leave home was a

beautiful one; a thousand diamonds glittered and sparkled on the crisp snow, as the bright light from the street-lamps fell upon it, and the temptation to spend an hour or two with his reckless companions before he left them was too strong to be put aside. So, carelessly remarking that he guessed he'd go over to the store for a while, he went out to spend his last evening with the wild young men whose acquaintance he had cultivated, and whose habits and manners he had long imitated. Reginald knew very well where he would be likely to find them; in fact, Will Green had suggested that day that he meet a few of the boys for a ''good-by treat'' at Reddy's Hotel in the evening.

The lad was not altogether hardened, and his conscience whispered to him not to heed the invitation, but to spend his last evening at home, especially as little Flossie begged him, just as he was going out, to hold her in his lap, and tell her about the big tigers in his natural history. But the evil angels prevailed. Down the streets he hurried, as if driven on by the spirits of darkness. The gay saloon, with its brilliant lights, is reached and entered. As he opens the door, snatches of vile songs and coarse laughter fall upon his ear. He does not intend to

13

stay long; but it takes only a glass or two to bewilder and confuse his mind, and the hours pass rapidly by, as in a dream. At last, as the midnight hour approaches, he is carried out by two of his companions, more accustomed to the effects of the vile cup, and steadied home, conscious only of an aching head, and an outraged stomach, and haunted by a vague fear of the results of his act of indiscretion. By the time he has dragged his unwilling feet up the steps, he is completely overcome, and is quite unable to enter the house. His sneaking companions, whom he calls "friends," ring the bell loudly, leave the poor lad in a heap upon the cold steps, and beat a hasty retreat.

Mrs. Beardsley had supposed that Reginald was at the store until his father came home at half-past nine; then she did not mention his absence, hoping her husband would not ask about him; and he, supposing Reginald had spent his last evening at home with his mother, said nothing. Mrs. Beardsley had two objects in expressing no surprise to her husband that Reginald was not with him when he came home; she hoped to be able thus to keep the truth from him, for she knew well that he would be grieved and disappointed that the boy had not kept his word, and perhaps he might refuse entirely to let him go to his uncle's. Even if he did not do this, she feared he would reprove him; and the unwise and foolish woman dreaded nothing so much as that her son, the darling of her heart, should receive censure for anything. She had gone to bed, hoping that he had taken a night-key with him, and that his father would not be awakened when he returned. She didn't believe in being so strict with him anyway, and was greatly annoyed because she could not induce her husband to give up his "straight-laced notions," as she termed them.

Let us not be too hard upon this woman, foolish and unwise as she appears. She believed in her son,— believed in him implicitly,—and that is well. No mother can have any influence over her son who does not believe in him. But Ellen Beardsley believed in her son blindly, unwisely, and against her better judgment; yes, even against the evidence of her own senses. She was getting to fear not so much the sin as the exposure; not so much the baneful effects of evil companions as that something should occur which would serve to thwart her cherished plans. She had not believed it possible that *her* boy could be led very far away from the path of rectitude; other boys might be led away, but surely not hers. Had she thought this possible, she would have been as greatly distressed and grieved as any less unwise mother. She hoped for great things from him—her first-born. He will graduate! How proud she will be of him! and how surprised Professor Hill will be! From this fond dream she was awakened by the loud ringing of the bell. Thoughts of Reginald were the first that filled her mind, and rushed in upon her waking consciousness, even as they had been the last that occupied her sleeping fancies.

"What is it, Ellen?"

"Nothing—just somebody at the door—that's all." A dread of something terrible about to happen almost paralyzed her tongue. What if—but no! it could not be Reginald. Still, she felt an unaccountable and almost overmastering desire to hurry down-stairs.

CHAPTER XVII

WHAT is it that sometimes, in hours of extreme danger, or moments of unusual trial, comes to us as with a message of warning—a premonition of impending trouble? Who can say but it may be the touch of the angel whose special mission it is to watch over us? who knows but it may be a faint whisper from his sacred lips, which reaches our inner consciousness, and in some mysterious manner impresses its message of warning upon our hearts?

"Wait, James! Let *me* go down—I *must* go!" she exclaimed, springing from her bed in nervous haste.

"Why, Ellen! I'll go, of course; what's the matter? you're nervous; you've been working too hard to get Regie ready to go. You'll be sick if you're not careful; now go back to bed; it's quite cold in the room. You need not be alarmed at all. I presume it's John Dillon on some little matter of business;

197

he often comes late, you know. I'll soon be back,"
he continued, reassuringly, from the top of the stairs.

Ellen Beardsley sank back on her pillow and listened. For a moment, that seemed an age to the
overwrought woman, she could hear nothing but the
loud beating of her own heart. Then she was sure
she heard Reginald's name and an exclamation of
astonishment from her husband.

It was but the work of a moment for the excited
woman to throw a shawl about her shoulders and follow her husband. She reached the door of the hall
just in time to see him partly lead and partly drag
a seemingly half-insensible form across the room to
the sofa.

"James! James! is it my boy? What has happened? What is it? tell me, Reginald! O, have pity
on me! Are you hurt? Has he been hurt, James?"

Her only answer was a stupid stare, accompanied
with an oath, and an unintelligible medley of words,
uttered with a thick tongue.

"Do I live to hear my son curse me? James!
James! I can not bear it!" moaned the wretched
woman, wildly wringing her hands, and falling upon
her knees by the side of the half-conscious lad. Already the nauseating smell of liquor has filled the

room, the warmth of which is beginning to tell on the poor boy with sickening effect.

Reader, let us draw a friendly curtain over this scene. Heart-breaking as it is, there is many a home that has witnessed its counterpart; many a mother's heart that has felt the numbing pain, the anguish unspeakable, that Ellen Beardsley felt that night. Many a loving father has trembled under a burden of like anguish, as he felt that he was draining to the dregs the cup of bitterness.

It is nearly noon of the next day before, thoroughly chagrined, the boy awakens. His head is aching still; but as he sees his well-packed trunk standing in the hall, his desire to go is as strong as ever. But he rightly judges that his father will be more determined than he has ever been not to trust him away from home. He is heartily ashamed of his conduct, and deeply regrets yielding to temptation. At last he decides that he will humble himself before his father, and ask him to forgive his folly when he comes home to dinner. This is an unusual resolution for the self-willed youth to form, but he sees no other way out of the trouble. Still he fears that his father will not have confidence enough in him to give him money, and allow him to go. If not, he decides so to work upon his mother's sympathies that she will give him the needed amount; or, should all else fail, he will help himself.

James Beardsley was gratified beyond words to see that his son appeared to sense the shame he had brought upon them, and listened eagerly to his expressions of sorrow and his fair promises. And, indeed, there was a deal of sincerity in them; for Reginald was not yet altogether hardened in evil, and his sorrow and shame over his conduct were not wholly feigned.

"Uncle Earl will expect me to start to-night, father," he urged; "and I can never do any better as long as I stay here; if I can only get away from the boys, I shall be all right."

"I guess he's right, James," said his mother, sadly. But it was plain to see that she did not speak with her usual assurance. For the first time in her life she questioned the wisdom of her course in training her son. So James Beardsley thought the matter over, and prayed over it earnestly, and finally decided that perhaps it would be as well for the boy to go.

Nevertheless, it was a sad home-leaving. Flossie sobbed convulsively; the strong, impulsive lad had always loved the little sister for her very weakness. She clung to him now, until papa unclasped the little white arms gently.

"Brother must go now, little sister. Good-by."

Then the child placed one tiny hand lovingly on the jetty locks, and said, tremulously: "Flossie's going to ask God to let a pretty angel go with Regie, and I guess it won't ever leave him."

"God grant it," said James Beardsley, earnestly.

Everything went on in about the old way after Reginald left; and now the snow and ice have melted away, and the early spring violets lift up their brave little faces cheerfully to the passer-by, as if to say: "See! here we are again. God is good; if He remembers us, surely He will not forget you."

Frequent letters from Reginald, and one occasionally from Uncle Earl, told pleasant stories of the absent boy's prosperity and of his success with his studies, until finally James Beardsley began to hope that his fears had been quite unfounded. But unaided human nature is utter weakness.

CHAPTER XVIII

THE REAPING TIME

ONE morning Grandmother Sharpe awakened with a severe pain in her side. She was almost always strong and well; and as is usually the case in such instances, she feared and dreaded the least symptom of disease, which she watched with wonderful solicitude. But as the weary hours dragged by, it became evident that the poor old woman's case was really serious. She rebelled all day against calling a doctor, on the ground that it would make her appear very ill. There was one thing rather remarkable about her—it mattered not how querulous and disagreeable she might be in health, it took but an hour or two of pain, or even of indisposition, to render her so kind and good-tempered that the contrast was wonderful. This instance was no exception to the rule. Whether it was fear of death that prompted these sudden reformations, or a real desire to make as little trouble as possible, no one could tell; but let us hope it may have been the latter.

On the morning of the second day of her illness, grandmother was so much worse that Mr. Beardsley insisted upon calling a doctor, who pronounced the case very serious. Mrs. Beardsley and Janet were kept busy all that day and the next, trying to ease her sufferings, but she rapidly grew worse, until it was plain that her mind was wandering. Grandpa Beardsley appeared to be continually in her thoughts.

"James," she would call, hoarsely, "James, see! your father wants a piece of toast. *I'll* make him some. Poor old man! see how white he looks. Don't—don't—Ellen—Regie!—don't speak so cross to him!" and then she would murmur, gently, "Saint of the Lord—poor old man!" Evidently grandmother was living over that never-to-be-forgotten day when the old deacon fell asleep.

At last, on the evening of the fifth day, she appeared to be sleeping quietly, and Mrs. Beardsley was trying to get a little rest, which she sadly needed. Suddenly about midnight, grandmother's shrill voice was heard calling in tones of anguish. Mrs. Beardsley hurried into the room, supposing her to be still delirious. In her agony, which appeared to be as much mental as physical, she raised herself up in her bed. Her black eyes gleamed like balls of fire, and she flung her arms wildly above her head. "Ellen! Ellen!" she cried, *"I'm goin' to die, and I ain't ready!* Where's James?"

"Would you like to have me send for Elder Maynard, mother? Shall I send Janet?"

"No! no! I want James to pray for me, Ellen. *He's* a Christian! Many's a time when he's been kind to me when I've been wicked an' spiteful. Call James, Ellen! O, how I wish I'd been better to his father," she added, with a sigh, as Mrs. Beardsley hurried to call her husband.

With hands raised to heaven, James Beardsley bowed beside the couch of the trembling woman; and with earnest voice and a heart filled with faith, he commended her to the keeping of the Good Shepherd, from whom none of His lambs ever wander so far that He can not hear their cry.

"Do you think He'll hear, James? *will* He hear?" she wailed. "O, I've been a 'wanton professor' so long! Bunyan calls 'em 'damnable.' If I'd been a better mother, Ellen, you wouldn't have found it such hard work to do right; but if you an' James'll forgive me, mebby the Lord will."

Ellen Beardsley was sobbing aloud. "Yes,

"Ellen! Ellen! I'm Goin' to Die, and I Ain't Ready!"

mother," she said gently, "we forgive you as we hope to be forgiven."

Quickly the restless head fell back on the pillows, the terrified expression in the deep eyes gave place to one of peace, and in a moment the sick woman dropped into a quiet slumber. It was as if the touch of healing had accompanied the assurance of pardon, even as when, nearly nineteen hundred years ago, the divine Master said to the dying sufferer, "Thy sins be forgiven thee; arise, and walk." When grandmother again awoke, the pain was gone, and an expression of such peace and happiness and love glorified her face that it was almost transfigured. "O Ellen! Ellen!" she cried, "the angels of God have met me!"

After that Grandma Sharpe gradually but surely regained her health and strength. But if those knowing her so well wondered within themselves if the keeping power of God would be strong enough for such as she, they gradually ceased to doubt as the weeks passed away. The jealous, unlovely disposition had been exchanged for one of kindness and loving charity toward all. In this wondrous change no one rejoiced more than did James Beardsley, and he often said to himself, "What hath God wrought!" Even the children noticed a difference in grandma.

"Dranma don't stold Bessie one bit all day," the child remarked in an astonished manner one afternoon when she had been unusually trying to grandma's patience: "Bessie just lites dranma now."

"Why, yes, Bessie," replied Flossie, in a whisper, "why yes; grandma says the angels met her one time, and one of 'em stays with her all day now; and I presume," she added, wisely, "it's the same one that stayed with grandpa 'fore he died; she acts most 'zactly like him."

Mrs. Beardsley's surprise at this change was very great; and, though she said little, the Spirit of God was pleading with her every moment. Night and day the burning words that her mother uttered in her mortal terror on that memorable night rang in her ears with ever-increasing frequency, and would not be dismissed: "I'm going to die, and I'm not ready!" What if the angel of death should again hover over their roof? what if *she* should be chosen? Would *she* be ready? At last her conscience was at work; and memory brought back many a scene, especially in the management of her children, which caused her much regret and pain. She remembered how unwisely she had dealt with Reginald; how she had failed to instruct him and warn him with loving tenderness;

what if *he* were never converted, as the result of her example and unwise course!

In the midst of reflections like these one beautiful morning in early summer the postman called with letters. There was one in the bold familiar hand of her brother Earl. She opened it with a dull foreboding of evil. It was a very brief letter; and as Ellen Beardsley read it with trembling haste, every word seemed to burn itself into her heart. She noticed that the wrapper was a square, pink-tinted one, instead of the plain white which her brother always made use of, and she dully wondered why he had used it. She even noted the scent of violets on the paper. Just then the canary began a merry tune from his cage in the sunny window, and she dimly realized that Janet was asking her some question about making a pudding for dinner. Strange that in moments of anguish, when the heart is suddenly filled with an overmastering sorrow, the most trivial affairs—the most commonplace sights and sounds— will stamp themselves upon the brain. Once more, with dry eyes and a feeling of suffocation at her heart, Mrs. Beardsley read the letter she had received. Let us stand by her side, and read with her the few brief words:

14

DEAR SISTER: Reginald left here this morning. I do not know just where he intended to go, but I think to some point in the South. We quarreled yesterday, Ellen, and this is the result. Of course, you will blame me; but when I tell you that I have just discovered that the young man has been appropriating money from my office for some time, I trust you will not think me hasty in allowing him freedom to go, as he naturally wished to do. I am much disappointed in him; for he seemed to be doing well at school. You will forgive me for saying that, although I am not a Christian, I must say I did not expect such duplicity from a boy who, I suppose, has had Christian precept and training from babyhood.

In much sympathy,

EARL.

With a second reading of the letter, the unhappy woman understood more fully its real import. She had only one thought—to hurry to her own room, where no one could witness her agony. She rose mechanically from her chair, and tottered forward; but her trembling feet refused to support her, and with a moaning cry, "My punishment is greater than I can bear!" she fell heavily to the floor.

For days the stricken woman lay upon her couch of pain, battling for life through the delirium of fever. Weary weeks of tedious convalescence followed,—weeks of heart-searching and deep humiliation of soul,—weeks when memory was busy bringing

"My Punishment Is Greater Than I Can Bear"

to her mind scenes which she would fain forget. She remembered with sorrow the unquestioned freedom she had given her son in the use of the too liberal allowance of money she had furnished him from childhood, until all sense of its true worth had been taken away; how she had screened him from blame in the matter of Janet's stolen money, and stubbornly refused to use reason or judgment.

She sees it all plainly now—the whole miserable affair. Tom Willis had told his story truly, after all—poor Tom! how she had wronged him! Knowing her son's dishonesty at last, she could understand many things that had puzzled her in the past. How blind she had been! how unjust to Tom! She decides to write and ask his forgiveness. She remembers her cruelty to little Tim Mallery; her unsympathetic, unloving conduct toward her noble husband; and last, but by no means least, her harshness and severity toward his godly father. All these things come up before her, and settle themselves with such crushing weight upon her soul that it seems to her she can never be forgiven.

In deep contrition of heart, Ellen Beardsley reviews her past life with all its deformity; but not until she fully realizes that the blood of Christ alone is sufficient to cleanse her sins; not until she flings herself, in her helplessness and sin, at the feet of the Saviour of sinners, and cries from her burdened heart, "Just as I am, . . . O Lamb of God, I come! I come!" does she feel the sweet peace of forgiveness; but when at last she arises from her bed of suffering, she is indeed a changed woman.

CHAPTER XIX

MAKING HOME PEACEFUL

MORE than eight years have passed since the events recorded in the preceding chapters took place. Ellen Beardsley's jetty hair is streaked with gray, and mourning for her wayward son has imparted a pathetic droop to her thin lips. Still through all these sorrowing years, the grace of God has been to her a mighty bulwark, a tower of strength. James Beardsley is happy in the thought that he is no longer *alone,* and in the sweet consciousness that the wife of his youth is walking with him the narrow path of peace; and, although sharing with her the terrible grief of mourning for the wayward son, from whom they have heard nothing but the most meager reports in all these years, he can say from his heart: "Blessed be the name of the Lord." "Though He slay me, yet will I trust in Him!"

Grandmother Sharpe appears actually younger than she did on the day when Reginald left home.

The small black eyes are filled with a kindly light,
and the shrill voice has somehow lost its harshness.
Baby Bessie is a tall, sweet-mannered, helpful little
maiden, thanks to the Christian training of the last
eight years.

Flossie,—I can see an eager, expectant look shining
in the eyes of my young readers at mention of this
name,—Flossie, patient, tender little Flossie, is the
same as of yore, only the passing years have given
an added grace to her manner, and an added beauty
to the almost classic features. She still loves to hear
stories of the angels, and believes with all her heart
that some kind messenger of the glory-land is watching over her big brother, and will some day bring
him back.

Janet still stays—a faithful creature—and poor
Mrs. Mallery, cheerful and grateful, lives in a tiny,
comfortable cottage, the happy pensioner of James
Beardsley.

*   *   *   *   *

Come with me now to a pleasant rural village
in the sunny South. It is late in December, but
the days are bright and warm, and the sweet scent
of roses fills the air. Everywhere they toss their
brilliant heads, vainly attempting, from their very

profusion, to gain the admiration that they richly deserve.

It is evening, and from the few pedestrians who are seen upon the streets, we judge that the hour is late. The street-lamps give a bright light in the better and more central part of the village; but the outskirts are deserted and quite dark, save for the soft light from the moon, which is near its full. The old bridge, which spans a small tributary of the mighty Mississippi, and leads from the village toward the east, is quite in the shadow. The note of a belated "chuck-will's-widow" is heard, which, with the monotonous swish of the river against the firm levees, is almost the only sound that breaks the stillness.

For some time the old bridge has been undergoing repairs, which have but recently been finished; and the temporary bridge for the workmen, consisting of only two or three narrow boards, laid at one side and extending to the middle pier, has not yet been taken down.

Look! along this improvised platform a man is making his way slowly and with uncertain steps. It takes but a second glance at the swaying figure to decide that he is intoxicated. See! he has reached the extreme end of the slender walk now, though

how he has accomplished the feat in his unbalanced
mental condition is a miracle. He stands for a
bewildered moment on the stone pier, for the walk
extends no farther. Quickly, as if dimly comprehend-
ing the state of affairs, he turns to retrace his steps;
his foot catches in the loose planks, there is a cry
of horror, a splash, and the dark waters close over
him. The cold water sobers him in an instant, and
he makes a hard struggle to reach the opposite bank.
But look! do you notice that heavy beam, just pro-
jecting from the surface of the water, like the back
of some cruel sea monster waiting for his victim?
It has caught the poor fellow in his downward flight,
and his right arm hangs limp and helpless at his
side. It is an unequal struggle. Visions of a pleasant
home, of a kind but overindulgent mother and a Christian father, and of a little golden-haired sister, float
like a changing panorama before his eyes. Again
he feels two tiny arms around his neck, and hears
a soft, sobbing voice close to his ear: "I guess the
pretty angel won't ever leave you." Then a white,
aged face and a bent form pass before his eyes; and
passages from the Book of God, repeated by the trembling lips, seem graven as with a pen of fire upon his
brain. He thinks of that summer evening—O, so

LOOK! ALONG THIS PLATFORM A MAN IS MAKING HIS WAY

long ago!—when his grandfather died, and the cruel words of a reckless lad, the last he ever spoke to the dear old man, ring mockingly in his ears. Then he thinks of the noble young man whom he so cruelly wronged, and wonders drearily where poor Tom is. A vivid panorama of his years of wandering and sin and shame, of the many times he had resisted the impulse to go home, like the poor prodigal, and beg forgiveness, passes before him. O, that he had heeded the voice of his good angel! Now it is too late! Is this to be the end? O, for one more opportunity to redeem the past! He seems to have lived a lifetime in one brief moment.

But help is at hand. A man is standing on the bridge. We have not seen him approach; but he must have heard that piercing cry of terror, and hurried to the rescue. In his hand he has a long rope, fortunately left by the workman upon the bridge. "Catch the rope! Hold on to the rope!" he cries; "steady!—look out for the timbers! That's good; we'll have you out of there in no time," he continues, cheerfully as with a strong hand he draws the drowning man steadily to the bank. The poor fellow is more dead than alive, and at first is unable to stand.

"I have broken my arm, I think, sir," he moans,

in a voice strangely familiar to us, "and I have no friends in the village—and—and," he faltered, "I have no money."

"Never mind that, never mind that; I'll have to play the part of the good Samaritan; for I'll not leave one of God's creatures to perish. Why that's my work, the work of my life, to help save poor souls. There's a friend of mine,—or at least I've known him for the few days that I've been in the village, and he's a noble Christian man, I believe, if ever one lived,— and I think he'll take you in until you're able to go home. Did you say you were going home?"

"Home!" the very word thrills the wanderer's heart! Going home! would they receive him?

"There's my friend's house, right over the bridge —that quaint old mansion, with a light in the window. They are waiting for me. I've been lecturing on temperance in the village, and already a few poor souls have been rescued, thank God."

They ascended the stone steps laboriously, for the bruised body and broken arm throbbed painfully, and rang the bell.

"Why, Mr. Blake; you are later than usual. I've been waiting for you; wife was tired, and has gone to bed. You must have found some personal work to do—why—has there been an accident? What is the trouble?''

At the sound of the familiar tone, the wanderer trembled, and shrank farther into the shadow.

''Well,'' explained Mr. Blake, ''I was providentially detained, and was just crossing the old bridge when I heard a cry. My friend here had fallen into the water; and as his arm seems to be seriously hurt, he will need care for some time. Was I right to bring him here?''

''Yes! God bless you, yes! What are we in this world for, if not to help one another! I'll call Maggie,'' and Mr. Willis stepped into another room. When he returned, the bright light was shining full into the young man's pain-drawn face. With a cry of surprise, his kindly host sprang toward him with extended hands: ''Reginald Beardsley! is it possible!''

''Yes, it's possible, Tom Willis; and now that you know who I am, I suppose you will curse me for a drunken dog, and turn me out to die!'' he exclaimed bitterly.

''God forbid! who am I that I should curse one for whom Christ died?''

At the mention of the name ''Beardsley,'' Mr.

Blake scrutinized the stranger's features sharply.

" 'Beardsley'? Young man, what—what is your father's name?"

"James Beardsley."

Mr. Blake turned, with an eager smile, and laid his hand almost caressingly upon the dripping, ragged sleeve. "So you are little Jimmie Beardsley's son. Praise the Lord! His ways are past finding out! Why, my boy, your Uncle Paul and I used to be fast friends—are yet, for that matter. He wrote me from India less than a month ago that he was soon coming home to surprise his brother. I used to know the whole family—noble family, too. The last time I saw your father, he was about your age. Didn't you ever hear him mention Sim Blake?"

"Yes, yes! O, sir! did you know my father?"

"From the time he was a little chap. O, I'd like to see Jimmie!"

"Come, Reginald," said Tom, "if you're able to step into the bath-room, I will help you get on something dry and warm. I've sent a boy after the doctor, who'll be here shortly; then we shall know the extent of your injuries. But whatever happens, remember you are to have a home here as long as you need one."

Reginald Beardsley was too humiliated to reply. He rose silently, and attempted to follow his host. Strange memories and stranger emotions rushed over him. He grew weak and faint, a sudden dizziness came upon him, and he fell to the floor.

When he awoke, kind voices sounded in his ear, and tender faces bent over him.

"I remember you said once," he sobbed, brokenly, to his host, "something about 'heaping coals of fire.' I didn't know what you meant then, but I do now. But how came you here? I thought you lived at Miles' Creek."

"Why, you see, uncle and aunt died some years ago; and then Maggie and I came a little farther South, where I found my good wife—how white you look! poor fellow!"

I need not tell you of the weeks of suffering the poor wanderer spent at the home of Tom Willis, who proved to be a true friend, but will only say that, like the prodigal son, he at length decides to go back to his father. He has tried the path of sin, and found it very grievous. He is sick of wandering, sick of sin and shame—sick of the old life. He has found it to be a life of vanity and vexation of spirit.

Wonderful is the love of God! Gracious is His

long-suffering Spirit! Slighted, abused, neglected for
years, it still pleads with a voice of infinite pity,
"My son, give Me thine heart."

At last, covered with humility as with a garment,
the wanderer yields. The infinite Love that has
followed him these weary years triumphs, and the
white-winged messengers, about the throne of glory
shout,—

"Rejoice! for the Lord brings back Him own!"

One afternoon early in March the postman stopped
at the old home in Harrisburg, and handed Mrs.
Beardsley a letter, addressed in her son's handwriting.
At the sight her hand trembled so she could not
open the envelope.

"Here, James, open it,—it's from Regie," she
gasped, and, almost as white as the masses of drifting
snow outside, sank into her chair.

The letter told of his years of wandering—it was
a long letter—and of his sin and shame and final
repentance; confessed his dishonesty at his uncle's,
and told of his determination to repay the amount
stolen from him; spoke of his injustice to Tom Willis,
and told how Tom had taken him in and cared for
him like a brother; and mentioned his rescue from
a terrible death, by his father's old friend, Sim Blake,

15

whom he had induced soon to accompany him home.

We will listen to the last paragraph of the letter:

Mother, I must return to Harrisburg, and redeem the past; and, as I have made the home of my parents a place of discord and unhappiness, I desire now, by God's grace, to unite with them and my sisters in the beautiful work of MAKING HOME PEACEFUL.

James Beardsley smiled through his tears as he glanced at the wife of his youth, upon whose face the peace of God rested like a benediction,—a face stamped by a character made perfect through suffering,—and said, reverently: " 'And My people shall dwell in a PEACEABLE HABITATION, and in sure dwellings, and in quiet resting-places.' 'And the work of righteousness shall be peace; and the effect of righteousness quietness and assurance forever.' "